The
Jesse Tree

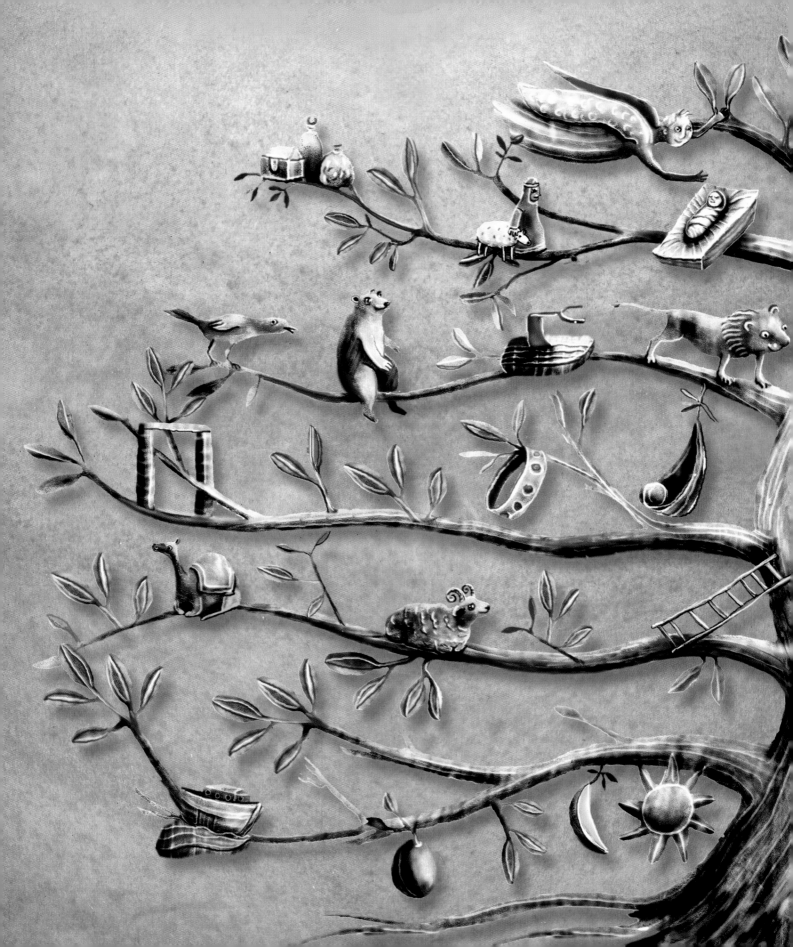

For my mother and father G.M.
To the tree, with gratitude B.W.

The
Jesse Tree

GERALDINE McCAUGHREAN
Illustrated by BEE WILLEY

LION
Children's Books

Published by
Lion Publishing plc
Mayfield House, 256 Banbury Road,
Oxford OX2 7DH, England
www.lion-publishing.co.uk
ISBN 0 7459 4577 5

First edition 2003
1 3 5 7 9 10 8 6 4 2 0

A catalogue record for this book is available
from the British Library

Typeset in 13/18 Elegant Garamond BT
Printed and bound in India

CONTENTS

INTRODUCTION

❧

In the old days, in the front of any family Bible, a record was kept of that family's history: the marriages, the children born of those marriages, the marriages and offspring of those children. Over the course of generations, those fading, spidery lines spread outwards, like branches and twigs from a single trunk. That is why we call such a record a "family tree".

Similarly, there would have been, in any number of churches, a "Jesse tree" – a depiction of Jesus' family tree in wood, or stone, or stained glass. Church garments might even have been embroidered with a tree.

Even thousands of years ago, when the stories of the Old Testament were first told, families were pictured as trees branching out from a single trunk.

"A shoot will spring from the stock of Jesse, and from his roots a bud will blossom," said the prophet Isaiah in the Bible, foretelling the birth of Jesus. It is this verse which gave rise to the tradition of Jesse trees in churches.

Jesse trees were the Bible-storybooks of unlettered people. A priest could point to the figures or symbols and tell the stories of those Old Testament kings, prophets, heroines, warriors. And the tree itself served to show how the New Testament grew out of the Old Testament; how, for Christians, the birth of Jesus was not just a beginning, but a completion. He was the flowering of a tree planted long before, by God's own design. By tracing his earthly ancestry back to King David and beyond, it was easy, too, to see Jesus as a real historical figure.

That forest of ancient Jesse trees fashioned in the Middle Ages is long gone. Puritan vandals of the seventeenth century, in their attempt to destroy all "graven images", smashed the heads from saints, the wings from angels, the figures from Jesse trees. No tree survives undamaged.

But, in recent times, a new tradition has grown up – a new strain of Jesse tree "grown" at home. Still planted for the sake of its stories, symbols are added day by day during the season of Advent, and day by day the old stories are retold, culminating in the stories of the first Christmas.

Whether you read the twenty-four stories in this book during Advent or enjoy it at one sitting, in the shade of a summer tree, remember that the Jesse tree's roots were put down centuries ago, and that its fruit is as sweet as ever.

THE JESSE TREE

"What are you doing, Mister?"

The old carpenter frowned. He hated people to watch him work. The big silence of the empty church suited him very well. When he saw the boy standing there, his frown turned to a scowl. "What are *you* doing in here?" he growled.

"I asked first."

The old man ran a creased hand over his half-completed woodwork. "I'm carving a Jesse tree, if you must know. Now run along out of here. A church isn't for playing in."

"Is that your name, then? Jesse?"

The carpenter was impatient to get on. "Of course not. A Jesse tree is a very ancient tradition. A thousand years ago, every church had a Jesse tree. A stained-glass window or a carved wooden screen… Nowadays, it's a lost art."

"No, it's not," said the boy. "You're doing it."

He wore a tee shirt and shorts: a holidaymaker, thought the old man with disgust. Trippers! They came to town, they made a mess, made a nuisance, then away they went. Small boys on holiday were the worst.

"Why a tree?" asked the boy.

The carpenter breathed out through his teeth. "It's like a family tree. You've heard of a family tree? Well, a Jesse tree is like that. It shows the ancestors of Jesus Christ, from the start of the world until his birth. You've heard of Jesus, I suppose?"

"I've heard of Jesus. Were the sun and moon his ancestors, then?" asked the boy, pointing to the carvings near the base of the tree.

"Of course not," snapped the old man. "Those are symbols. They mark the start of the story. The beginning."

"I like stories," said the boy.

"Go and watch TV, then."

But the boy did not go. He sat down on a pew. "Have you forgotten the story?" he asked after a moment.

"Huh! You should know it already, ignorant child. When I was your age, we knew all the stories in the Bible. These days…"

"So tell me," said the boy.

And there was nothing for it but to tell him the story behind the carvings of the sun and moon.

PARADISE GARDEN

First there was the idea, complete and perfect: the beginning, the end and everything in between. (God is a craftsman, you see, and a craftsman always plans before he begins work.) Then God flexed his fingers and began. He made light and with it warmth and beauty (because you can't see beauty in the dark). He took all the makings in his two palms – energy, gases, liquids and solids – and when he had finished, there was the world, spinning in and out of sunlight, with the moon to light the dark hours.

He put fish in the seas and animals on land and, in the loveliest spot of all, he planted a garden. Last of all, he made a gardener – made him out of clay – prettier than a sloth, not as marvellous as an angel; somewhere between the two. That was Adam: First Man.

To keep Adam from being lonely, God took one of Adam's ribs, and from it he made Eve – First Woman – smoother, softer, smaller. But in one special way, Adam and Eve were not like the other animals: when God breathed life into them, he passed on a little something of himself. ❧

"A family likeness, you mean. I get you. My mum says I look like my grandma," said the boy. "But why the sun and moon? Why didn't you carve Adam and Eve?"

"I told you, boy. These are symbols. They represent the time when God began his great plan. As it happens, Adam and Eve almost ruined everything… But people who come into this church will look at this sun, this moon, and remember how God created the world."

"And now you are creating it all over again," said the boy.

The old man was so angry that his fist tightened around his chisel and he shook it. "Don't talk wickedness, boy! I don't liken myself to God! That'd be falling into the sin of pride, that would!"

The boy looked startled. "Why? You said it yourself: there's a likeness. A family likeness. It's just that you're using wood, not clay. Go on with the story."

"I'm not here to tell stories!" raged the old man. "I'm here to work – if I'm left in peace."

"Is that what Adam and Eve did? Stop God working? You said they nearly ruined everything. What did they do?"

The old man felt cornered, as if a dog had pinned him against the wall of the great empty church. He looked towards the door for a mother or father who might come and call the boy off. No such luck. ❧

"There is everything here in Paradise Garden that you will ever need," said God to Adam and Eve. "Food, shelter, birdsong. Me. Eat whatever you want – strawberries, mangoes, honey, anything. Just don't eat from the tree in the middle of the garden – the tree of knowledge."

It was a test, you see; a test of their love for God.

Suddenly, of course, there was nothing so interesting to Adam and Eve as that tree in the middle of the garden. Why was this one different from the rest? How? Time and again, Adam and Eve were drawn back to stare at the forbidden fruit of the tree of knowledge.

"Eat," said a voice to Eve. "Taste and then you will know. Why else is it called the tree of knowledge?" A beautiful creature with shimmering scales and a forked tongue crept out from among the roots. "Eat. Then you will know as much as God himself."

It was a test, you see, of whether they would put themselves or God first. With a delicious shudder of excitement, Eve picked a juicy piece of fruit and bit into it. Adam ate too. Bitter. No great wisdom descended on them. All they knew was that they should not have done it. They looked down, and their slender brown bodies looked nasty and rude.

"Now look what you've done, woman! Cover yourself up!" snapped Adam.

"You too! You too!" Eve complained.

God knew at once, of course. They could hide among the bushes, stitch clothing out of leaves, but God knew. Suddenly the birds in Paradise Garden sang out of key.

"Why did you disobey me?" God asked sadly. "Now you will have to go. The garden can no longer offer you a home. Don't come back until you have found my forgiveness."

So Adam and Eve were driven out of the garden and began a long, hard journey that lasted all their lives and much, much longer. Their children and their children's children went looking for the way back to Paradise Garden, but none of them could find it. They all disobeyed God, too – some in much worse ways than Adam and Eve's. Much worse. God had a rescue plan, of course. One day he planned to send…" ❧

"So what happened to the garden?" the boy interrupted.

The question took the old man by surprise. "God set an angel at the gate with a fiery sword – *to keep out trespassers*," he added pointedly.

"But what happened to the tree of knowledge? Did God chop it down?"

This was insufferable. "I don't know! Maybe. Why should he? It's lost to us, at any rate. You and I will never see it."

The boy got up and came closer to examine the knobbly roots of the carved Jesse tree. "That's why you are planting a new one."

The old carpenter grunted his disgust. "Haven't you been listening to a word I said? I told you – this is a *Jesse* tree, not the tree of knowledge."

"It's teaching *me* plenty," said the boy.

Then he was gone.

A Boat Full of Animals

"Get it out! Get it out!"

Startled by the shout, the wet dog standing beside the boy began to bark. The noise rang round the church.

"What are you thinking about, bringing an animal into the church!"

"It's raining," said the boy. The dog shook itself and water drops spattered them both. "Don't you like dogs?"

"Isn't it bad enough to have death-watch beetle eating away at the roof without having wet dogs, too?"

"I like boats," interrupted the boy.

The carpenter scowled down at his latest carving. "It's not a boat, you ignorant child. It's an ark."

"It has no funnels. How did it go?"

"It didn't have to *go*. All it had to do was float."

The dog suddenly lay down, like a collapsing sandcastle, its eyes glistening and its ears cocked. Now two of them wanted a story!

Too many boys making a nuisance of themselves. I expect that was half the trouble… As the world filled up with the sons and granddaughters and great-great-great-grandchildren of Adam and Eve, it got worse instead of better. In fact, God decided he had been wrong to create the human race at all. The earth crawled with wickedness – like when the flying ants swarm.

Noah was different. A good man. He kept his tools clean, kept his conscience clear. God liked Noah.

"Noah," said God. "A flood is coming. It will wash away every living thing – wash the earth clean again. But you and your family are my friends: I wish you no harm. Do exactly as I say…"

Now, this was a dry, hot part of the world, a long way from the sea. When Noah's neighbours saw him building a ship, they sniggered and held out their palms and squinted at the sky. "What's the ship for, Noah? Expecting rain? Tee-hee."

Noah's ark was huge, with three decks and a roof over all.

"Why so big, Noah? Expecting visitors?" snorted the neighbours, and scrawled on the hull with lumps of chalk.

Then the animals started to come: lions and lynxes and leopards. The neighbours stayed away after that. There were warm-blooded and cold-skinned beasts, furry and feathered, smooth and scaly. There were crawlers and leapers, grazers and scavengers, wild and tame. There were creatures with names and ones so odd that only God knew what they were called. Inside the ark, they shifted, whined and gibbered. There were males and there were females: one of each. There were butterflies and even birds.

"Why birds, God?" wondered Noah. "Surely birds can fly into the treetops when the flood comes."

But when the flood came, there were no treetops. Rain fell from the sky like a waterfall, uprooting trees and boulders and towns. Noah's wife and family went aboard the ark and shut the doors. The darkness inside was warm with animals, sweet with animal breath. Things skittered unseen across the floor. Rain thudded on the roof.

The neighbours beat on the hull. "Let us in, you – !"

The rivers filled, burst, joined. The distant sea came ashore. The ark grated, rolled, pitched, spun, and was washed away like a coconut carried out to sea. Inside the ark, the animals blinked at Noah. The drumming of the rain wiped out every other sound.

The tarry planks kept out the daylight. Aboard the ark, day and night were the same colour. The animals slept and woke. The smell was soon as thick as mud.

Only after forty days and forty nights did the rain stop. But when Noah lifted off the hatches, he saw only sun and sky and water. There were no treetops – not even any mountaintops. Litter floated by: a shoe, a basket, a wooden spoon.

The wet ark steamed. The water dimpled. Bubbles rose. A fish jumped: the
only sign of life. It was the beginning of the world again. Somewhere in the ark,
a blackbird started to sing.

Weeks passed. The ark stank. The elephants swayed listlessly from foot to foot.
Now, surely, the flood *must* be drying up.

"Fetch me a raven," said Noah.

The raven cruised out over the water, its reflection like a black fish. But it found
nowhere to land.

Next, Noah sent a dove. But after a while it returned; it had found the world
still underwater. Seven days later, Noah sent the dove out again. When it came
back, it held in its beak a tiny olive twig. Somewhere, an olive tree must be poking
its branches through the shining water! Next
time Noah loosed the dove, it did
not come back at all.

With a grinding shudder, the ark ran aground on a mountaintop. The animals growled and bellowed, squealed and chattered and spat. Noah's daughter-in-law stroked her round stomach; her baby would after all be born on dry land. New life in a new world. The water and the sky and the breeze and the light whispered, "Never again!"

Mud squelched under the hooves of a horse that picked its way across the sodden ground. "Now we must get things right," said Noah, "or next time…"

Suddenly, it was as if the sky remembered colour. A great triumphal arch of streaming colour bridged the sky from horizon to horizon. "Never again," whispered God. "Never again will I drown the earth," and he signed his promise with the world's first rainbow. ❧

The rain had stopped. Sunlight streamed through the stained-glass windows and cast a rainbow over the wet dog. "So, Noah *must* be Jesus' ancestor, right? Because there was no one else left after the flood?"

"That's what some people say," muttered the carpenter.

"So Noah must be your ancestor, too, come to that. And mine. That makes us relatives!"

"Oh, now, wait a moment…"

"Did people do better the second time around?" asked the boy.

"Not so you'd notice," grunted the carpenter, and went back to carving the waves beneath his oaken ark.

"Was that God's rescue plan, then?" asked the boy. "You said he had a rescue plan. Bit drastic. Wipe everybody out and start again."

"No, no! Well, yes, but no." The carpenter looked confused. "In the long run, God was planning to send Jesus. That's the rescue plan I was talking about…"

But the boy was busy with his own thoughts. "Were there death-watch beetles on the ark, do you think?"

"Definitely not! Perishing little pests!"

"There must've been. Or they wouldn't be here now," said the boy.

"Get that dog out of here and don't bring it back! I don't know what things are coming to! Dogs in the Lord's house, indeed!"

STRANGE VISITORS

There was no dog with the boy when he came the next day. There was a little boy instead.

"You mean there are *more* of you?" said the old man with a despairing sigh.

"He was lost. I said I'd show him the way back to the caravan park." He turned to the smaller boy. "There's the Jesse tree I told you about. There's the sun and moon, there's the boat, and now he's doing a horse."

"It's not a horse. It's a camel," snapped the carpenter.

"Did it get left behind by Noah? Is it wading? It's got no legs."

"It's sitting down. Resting in the desert. It stands for… I mean, it's a symbol for Abraham."

"Was Abraham a camel, then?"

The old man scowled such a scowl that both boys ought to have melted then and there. But they didn't. "Sit down," the boy advised his friend. "He's going to tell us the story of Abraham now."

Abraham was a nomad; he did not belong anywhere. His tent was like the ark floating on the flood – one day here, another day there. When the goats and sheep had eaten all the grass in one place, Abraham and his wife, Sarah, moved on. They did not mind. God was good to them. The only regret they had was their lack of a son. Year after year they had longed for a child. Too many years. Now Sarah was too old. It seemed that, when Abraham and Sarah died, their tent and sheep and camels would pass to strangers. ❧

"Yes? Go on," said the boy. "Why did you stop?"

"I never meant to start," said the old man gruffly, polishing his chisel on the tail of his shirt. But he went on even so. ❧

Then one day, three figures walked out of the low light. The heat made their shapes waver.

Sarah was inside the tent, preparing food, but Abraham beckoned to them. "Come! Eat! Drink! Rest, strangers!"

"You are a hospitable man, Abraham. May your son bring you great joy. Children do."

"We have no child," said Abraham. "My wife, Sarah…"

"… will have a son," one stranger interrupted. "And that son will be the father of many sons."

Inside the tent, Sarah heard this and laughed to herself: a soft, bitter, inward laugh.

"Why did Sarah laugh?" asked another of the strangers. "Doesn't she know that with God all things are possible?"

The tent trembled, and suddenly Sarah stood in its doorway, staring. They could not possibly have heard her laugh! How could they know a thing like that? How could they? A group of strangers…

The visitors drank goat's milk, broke bread with Abraham and walked on. The desert dust swallowed them up. The heat broke the setting sun

into white crumbs of light. The first star of evening was rising.

"Can you believe it?" gasped Sarah, half-laughing, her hand resting on her stomach.

"I can," said Abraham. "I do. I've told you before how God spoke to me once – years ago – and said, 'Abraham, your descendants will be as numberless as the stars in the sky.' I should not have needed three strangers to tell me. I should have known: God always keeps his promises." ❧

"And Abraham is one of Jesus' ancestors, right, and that's why you're carving his camel on the Jesse tree?"

"Correct."

"So Jesus was going to be one of Abraham's many, many, many, many countless-as-the-stars descendants, right?" said the boy.

"Yes, yes." The old man tossed his head irritably, as if these things were too complicated for boys to understand.

"The brightest one."

"Yes, yes. The brightest one. Can a working man get no peace these days?"

A TEST OF LOVE

"This is my little brother. He cut himself." The voice was all too familiar to the carpenter, who gave a glum sigh. "I took him to the First Aid station on the beach. But I thought you could cheer him up with a story. The sheep's new."

"It's a ram," said the old man, running a rough palm over his latest carving.

The little brother curled up on a pew to listen. ❧

When Sarah gave birth to a son – (oh yes, God kept his promise) – Abraham called him "Isaac", which means "he laughed". The child must have taken after his mother, you see. Isaac was a fine boy – not like some you see nowadays. He was helpful to his mother, did as he was told, was good with the animals, and was brave and handsome and clever. To Abraham and Sarah, he seemed even more special, because they had waited so long for him. That is what made it all the harder…

The morning was cold, but there were beads of sweat on Abraham's neck as he lashed a bundle of firewood to the donkey's back. "Fetch me a big knife, Isaac, and a coil of rope. We have to go into the mountains and offer a sacrifice to God."

It was not unusual. In those days, people often made burnt offerings on their altars: the first sheaf of harvest, the best lamb from the flock. It was a way of thanking God for his goodness.

"Where are you going, Abraham?" said Sarah, snatching at his arm. "Why is your face so pale?" But Abraham would not answer. The donkey seemed unwilling to move: it leaned back against the bridle.

But at last they were on their way up the mountain paths – Isaac carrying a lighted brand, Abraham tugging the donkey along.

"Oh! Have we forgotten the lamb for the sacrifice?" asked Isaac, hoping they would not have to turn back.

"God will provide that," said Abraham. His face was as empty as a broken jug. They did not talk after that.

The highest places are the holiest. Abraham climbed up very high indeed. Then he piled up the firewood, turned awkwardly and wrapped his arms round his son. It was something between a hug and a grab. "It's you, son! God wants you for the sacrifice!"

No laughter now from Isaac.

Abraham bound him with the rope, and laid him on the altar. The knife in one hand, he placed the other over his son's face – over his eyes. His fist rose to make the blow. Quickly now, quickly. Get it over. Done. Get it done… The tears in his eyes made rainbows of everything…

"Abraham! Abraham!" The voice came from nowhere and from everywhere. "Stop! Enough. Look."

A nearby thorn bush shook. An animal bleated. A ram had tangled its horns in the bush and couldn't get free. Together father and son dragged it to the altar and offered it up to God. Its blood stained them both.

It had been a test, you see: to prove whether there was anything – anyone – Abraham loved more than God; whether there was anything he would try to keep back from God. ❧

"But you've carved the ram – not Abraham or Isaac. People might think Jesus was descended from a sheep. You know, the one that had to die."

"Don't be ridiculous."

The little brother had fallen asleep along the pew, his cut hand folded across his throat. They both stood looking down at him.

"I couldn't," said the boy. "Could you?"

"Could I what?"

"Pass the test. Kill your son."

Suddenly the angry carpenter was brandishing his chisel, high up over their heads, for all the world like a big knife. *"I don't have a son!"*

"Ah," said the boy, unperturbed. "Maybe that's why you don't laugh much."

After they were gone, the old man returned, grumbling, to his work. But the words kept chipping at his brain, in time with the tapping of his mallet. The sheep that had to die. Jesus: the sheep that had to die.

STAIRWAY TO HEAVEN

"I had a dream last night."

The old man jumped. Could the boy not cough politely or say, "Excuse me"? Must he just suddenly be there, talking? It scattered the old man's thoughts like birds out of a tree.

"I dreamed I was Jack, climbing the beanstalk."

"I only have nightmares," said the carpenter.

"Was one of Jesus' ancestors a fireman?"

"Certainly not... why?"

"Well, where's that ladder going?" He came and put his small fingers on the rungs of the ladder that stood propped mysteriously among the leaves of the carved Jesse tree.

"Don't meddle," said its maker.

The little fingers climbed the ladder, rung by rung. "Tell me." ❧

Everything about Jacob was smooth, from his well-washed skin to the words in his mouth. Only his wits were sharp. His mother thought the world of him. His father, Isaac, preferred Esau, though. Esau was rough and tough; as different as sacking from silk – and Esau was his firstborn son.

Esau and Jacob were twins, born only moments apart, but in those days it mattered very much who came first into the light of day. So Esau was his father's heir and Jacob wasn't. When Isaac died, Esau would become head of the family and Jacob wouldn't. That one thought chafed, like sacking against silk.

Esau was a hunter, forever chasing deer across the plains and through the snaggling woods. Jacob preferred to stay at home. His mother liked to have him near her. Also he had plenty of time to think.

One day, Esau came home half-dead with weariness. He flung himself down, muddy from head to foot and with twigs in his hair. "Give me something to eat, Brother. I'm done in."

Quiet as a woman, Jacob glided to the fire and filled a wooden bowl with stew. Its savour filled the room, rich and delicious. "You give me your birthright," he said teasingly, "and I'll give you the stew."

"Hurry up. I'm starving to death," complained Esau.

"It's yours… in return for your birthright."

"What d'you mean, my birthright? Give me the stew, can't you?"

"From now on, I'm the firstborn. That's all."

Esau wagged a weary hand. "Whatever you say." After all, how could a bowl of stew make a difference to the facts? Esau had seen the light of day first. He wolfed down the stew and fell fast asleep.

But Jacob held him to the deal. By the time Esau woke, everyone knew that he had sold his place as Isaac's heir in return for a bowl of stew. His only comfort? He was still his father's favourite son. His father's blessing would surely come to him.

"Hunt a deer and cook its meat for me," whispered old Isaac one day, frail as a cobweb, as blind and chilly as ice. "Then I shall give you my dying blessing."

Now, in those days, a father's blessing was considered as powerful as a wish granted. Away went Esau to catch his deer. In slid Jacob, subtle as a cat, his forearms covered in strips of hide, his borrowed clothes smelling of the woods. (His mother had put him up to it.)

"Here you are, Father. It's me, Esau. I brought you the venison you asked for."

Isaac took the bowl of tender meat from Jacob – as unsuspecting as Esau
had been when he had taken the stew.

"My boy," the old man said, feeling the coarse, hairy hands that
clasped the bowl. "Let me kiss you. My blessing is yours." And thus,
for a second time, Jacob stole from his brother.

When Esau found out how he had been cheated, he begged
Isaac to bless him too.

"My blessing is given," said the old man, sharing his
son's sorrow.

Esau was so angry that Jacob had to run for
his life – out into the countryside where he
had never hunted, out into the woods
where the deer knew the way better
than he did, out under a scowling sky.
Who knows why God forgave
Jacob – the trickster, the cheat –
except that God forgives most things.
Who knows why God leaned out
of heaven and kissed Jacob on his
smooth forehead? But he did.
That night, Jacob lay down to
sleep, with only a rock for a
pillow, and he had the
strangest dream of
his life.

He dreamed he saw a bright hole in the sky above him – as if he were lying on the bottom of a frozen lake, looking up through a hole in the ice. And stretching down from the hole was a ladder – the longest ladder imaginable, and as broad as a flight of stairs. Figures of snowy brightness were climbing the ladder, their faces brushed by the hems of yet more figures climbing down from above.

Angels.

"Jacob," said a voice within his dream. "Just as I promised your grandfather, Abraham, I am going to make you the father of a great people, and bring them into a land of their own."

Even when Jacob woke, the dream lingered behind in his eyelids, like a flash of lightning. He knew that God had spoken to him. He knew that being a part of God's plan would cost him more than a bowl of stew or a dish of meat. He knew that God would ask more from him than tricks and a quick wit. He was filled with excitement and joy and terror and shock, all at once.

Above all, he longed to tell his twin brother… but of course, that was out of the question. One day, one day, he would have to put things right with Esau. ❧

"I suppose, if your Jesse tree was tall enough, the angels could shin up and down that," said the boy.

"Don't talk daft," said the old man.

But, funnily enough, that night, he dreamed that his Jesse tree had grown like some magic beanstalk all the way up into the sky, and that day-trippers were climbing up and down it, their mouths white with ice cream and laughter.

29

THE DREAMER

"You've been fighting!" exclaimed the carpenter the next day, when the boy came into the church. "Typical!"

"My brother wanted my baseball cap. So he took it. He's bigger than me… But I got my own back!"

"I'll bet you did. Tit for tat. Knock for knock. That's all you kids understand these days…"

"Yes, I was going to bring him here. But after he took my cap, I didn't. So he won't get to hear the story, will he?"

"What story?"

"The one about that pyjama jacket," said the boy, pointing.

"It's not a pyjama jacket!" protested the carpenter hotly, in defence of his latest carving. "It's Joseph's coat-of-many-colours!" &

Jacob married and had twelve sons. Twelve! The eleventh – young Joseph – was a delightful boy. At least, Jacob thought so.

Joseph was a dreamer – not a daydreamer but a night-dreamer who remembered his dreams when he woke. "Last night I dreamed we were harvesting, and your sheaves bowed down to my sheaf," he told his eleven brothers. His brothers did not think much of his dream.

"Last night I dreamed we were all stars in the sky and that you eleven stars all bowed down to me." Joseph's brothers did not want to hear this either.

"Look what Father gave me!" said Joseph, wagging the sleeves of a glorious new coat. "Look at all the colours! Look at the cloth!"

Joseph's brothers did not want to look. No father ought to love one son more than all the rest – or if he does, he ought not to let it show. They hated Joseph for his coat and his dreams and his unfair share of love.

So one day, when Joseph brought them their lunch – way out in the hills, out of sight of home – they grabbed him, tore off the fancy coat and threw him into a pit.

Like a crumpled rainbow the coat was laid at old Jacob's feet. "A terrible accident, Father!" they said. "Dear little Joseph… Some wild animal… All we found was

this… He must be dead." Then the grief in Jacob's eyes made their lies peter out to a sorry silence.

But Joseph was not dead. Even hating him the way they did, his brothers had stopped short of murder. They had gone back to the pit, arguing about what to do with him. As they argued, a caravan of camels clanked by, bound for Egypt. "Let's sell him for a slave!" suggested Judah. And as they watched their hated brother led away, stumbling, dirt-coloured, in the dust behind the camel train, it really seemed that Fate had taken a hand.

Fate had. 🖎

Suddenly, realizing what a long story he had begun, the carpenter pulled himself up short. "I haven't got time for this! I've got work to do."

"All right. I'll come back tomorrow for the rest. But promise…"

"Promise? I don't have to pro–"

"… if my big brother comes by, don't tell him that story. It might give him ideas."

FAMINE AND PLENTY

"I suppose he came back?" said a voice the next day. "It wouldn't be much of a story if Joseph…"

"Much of a story? Much of a story? The Bible wasn't written to entertain you, you know!" The chisel trembled in the leathery old hands. "And no, Joseph didn't come back. He stayed in Egypt. He had a gift, didn't he? God had given him a gift. Joseph understood dreams – not his own, maybe, but other people's dreams."

In Egypt, things went from bad to worse. Although Joseph worked hard, he ended up in prison, convicted of a crime he had not committed. He felt hopeless and lost. But in Egypt, people valued dreams and dreaming. When his fellow prisoners had nightmares, Joseph explained what the dreams meant; he was always right. The prisoners were astounded, but they forgot Joseph, of course, the moment the sunlight shone in their eyes again.

Luckily, when the pharaoh – the ruler of the country – was himself plagued with dreams that none of his advisors could interpret, someone remembered the Hebrew slave rotting in the city gaol. "Send for him!" said Pharaoh, black-eyed for want of sleep.

"You dreamed of cattle clambering out of the Nile," said Joseph, as he knelt before the throne. "First seven sleek, fat cows, then seven bony, thin ones. The thin ones gaped their throats and swallowed down the fat."

Pharaoh flinched from the memory of his dream. "But what does it *mean*? Can you tell me that, Hebrew?"

"For seven years, Egypt's harvest will be marvellous – the granaries full of grain. But for seven years after that, every harvest will fail and your people will go hungry – unless you take steps to prevent it."

So impressed was Pharaoh, so taken with this dream-reader, that he made Joseph governor of Egypt. From then on, Joseph spoke on the pharaoh's behalf and was almost as powerful as the pharaoh himself.

The dreams had come from God, of course. So too did the seven years of plenty. Joseph gave orders for all the surplus food to be stored in great granaries and for nothing to go to waste. Sure enough, there followed seven years of famine, but, thanks to Joseph's careful planning, no one in Egypt starved.

Far away in Joseph's homeland, the sheep shook on their thin shanks. The brothers' stomachs were empty. "Go into Egypt where the granaries are full," said their father, Jacob, "and buy grain." (His old face, drooping like the wax from a candle, had not smiled since the day they brought him Joseph's multicoloured coat stained with blood.)

So that is how Joseph came to see his brothers again – kneeling in his chamber of state, asking permission to buy grain from the great Egyptian granaries. They did not know him, of course. He wore Egyptian robes, an Egyptian wig; his eyes were black-rimmed with Egyptian kohl. Besides, twenty years had passed since the business of the coat, the pit, the merchant caravan… But Joseph knew his brothers, oh yes, all ten of them…

Ten? Where was the eleventh? Where was little Benjamin, the youngest?

Joseph questioned them, demanded to know why one brother had stayed behind. To their dismay, he sent them home to fetch Benjamin. "But our father!" they protested. "He relies on Benjamin! His whole life is bound up in the boy. If anything were to happen…" They might as well have been talking to the pyramids themselves. Joseph was adamant.

So Benjamin was fetched, and the brothers were allowed to load their pack animals with good grain and to set off, marvelling at the generosity of that governor of Egypt, marvelling at the splendour of the Egyptian civilization.

Then the soldiers came after them, stopped them and began to search. "We took nothing! On our lives, nothing!" protested the brothers. "If you find anything on one of us, let the culprit be put to death!" How they must have regretted those words when the guards reached into Benjamin's saddlebag and pulled out the silver cup and brandished it in their faces. "Not Benjamin! Benjamin would never…" Their hands fell helpless by their sides. Their knees failed under them.

Joseph (who had given orders for the silver cup to be planted among their belongings) looked on with grim satisfaction. His brothers were as afraid now as Joseph had been twenty years before when, wrists tied, he had stumbled into slavery behind the merchant camel train. Childhood dreams swam before Joseph's eyes – their sheaves of corn flattened before his own; their stars dimmed by his brilliance. And Joseph went into a side room and wept – for all the lost years, for all the broken dreams, for the marvellous and confusing ways in which God worked out his plan.

When Joseph revealed his true identity to his brothers, there were no reproaches, no apologies, only tears of joy and relief and healing. Jacob was sent for – a frail old man rattling his weary bones over dusty roads to be reunited with the son he had thought dead for twenty years.

And Jacob's family was not alone in finding a new home in a new country. Many more Hebrews travelled to Egypt to escape famine and stayed on there as settlers along the fertile Nile. God had promised to take care of them, and perhaps this move to Egypt was his way of doing it. Let the Egyptians worship their boatload of animal-headed gods; the Hebrews would stay loyal to their one God. After all, they were his chosen people – his favoured sons and daughters. Surely they were the ones to whom he would give the best gifts, the ones he could not help but love the best. ❧

"You say that as if it turned out different," said the boy.

"It did," said the carpenter. "Within a few generations, life in Egypt all went horribly wrong for the Hebrews."

"So God broke his promise?"

"He never promised life would be easy, only that he would stay close to his people – the children of Israel."

"You can tell me tomorrow."

The old man gave an irritable groan. As the church door slammed shut behind his visitor, he called after him, "No promises!" but probably too late to be heard.

"LET MY PEOPLE GO!"

"So what went wrong in Egypt?" It was a small voice, but it filled the big church. The boy came and stood at his elbow. "I'm hungry. The ice cream van didn't come today. Is that a whip you're carving? Did one of Jesus' ancestors drive a stagecoach?"

"I am carving a whip to symbolize the time when the Hebrews – the Israelites, that is – were slaves. As the years passed, Joseph and the famine were forgotten. A new pharaoh was in power. Then the Egyptians suddenly looked around at the huge number of Hebrews living in Egypt and took fright. So they made the Hebrew settlers their slaves and worked them like pack animals or farm beasts."

"But God had a rescue plan, I'll bet."

"Naturally."

"Jesus!"

"Noooo, no no no no! Ignorant boy. This was long, long before Jesus. This time, God saw that his chosen people were in trouble and he sent Moses."

"Did he help them escape? Cool! Tell us!" ❧

Moses could not believe his eyes. A bush was burning – and yet it was not. As if extra leaves on the twigs, yellow and red flames covered the bush, but did not destroy it. Then, strangest of all, a voice spoke, out of the bush: "Take off your shoes, Moses. You are standing on holy ground."

Moses shuffled out of his sandals, never once taking his eyes off the burning bush.

"I am the God of your ancestors, the God of Abraham, Isaac and Jacob. I have heard the voice of the children of Israel crying out to me for help. So go to Egypt, Moses, and tell the pharaoh to let my people go."

These were not words Moses wanted to hear. Oh, he was an Israelite himself, and he knew very well what they were suffering. He had grown up in Egypt – not as a slave but in the pharaoh's own palace, adopted by the pharaoh's daughter. Just once he had stood up for his fellow countrymen – he had killed an overseer who was beating a Hebrew slave to death with a whip. For that, Moses had had to flee from Egypt as a hunted criminal.

"I can't. I'm sorry. You're asking the wrong –"

"You shall. I have chosen you to speak for them and to fetch my people out of slavery. Find your brother, Aaron, and take him with you if you feel the need of his eloquence. I shall be with you both. Go."

So Moses gave up his safe little life, tending sheep, and went back to Egypt where his fellow Israelites toiled all day under Egyptian whips.

"The God of Israel says, 'Let my people go,' " said Moses nervously. Pharaoh laughed and, to punish his insolence, gave orders that the slaves in the brickfields should make bricks without the straw they needed for the task.

"Let my people go," said Moses, while Aaron worked small wonders, turning a stick into a snake.

"A magic trick," Pharaoh scoffed.

"Let my people go, or the God I serve will do terrible things to make you change your mind."

But Pharaoh only curled his lip in contempt.

Then plagues like the strands of a slave-master's whip fell across Egypt. The Nile turned to blood. Frogs by the million made fat red blots as they hopped ashore out of the crimson river or rained down out of the sky.

"Let my people go!" said Moses, but Pharaoh would not.

The frogs died in the street and black flies rose off them in swarms. A plague of flies. God sent diseases that shrank all the fat sleek cows, horses, camels into bony bags of hide. He plagued smooth Egyptian bodies with lice and boils and rashes. The crops died in the fields.

"Let my people go," said Moses, but Pharaoh would not.

So God browbeat Egypt with fiery hail and freak storms, and sent locusts to eat up all the crops.

"Now will you let my people go?" said Moses.

But Pharaoh said, "No."

The last plague was the worst of all. God sent the angel of death – dark as the storm, sharp as the hail, sickening as frogs or boils, winged like a locust, fearful as a blood-red river. Each Israelite family smeared its doorpost with lamb's blood, and at the sight of that the angel turned away. But under every Egyptian door, shut or open, locked or barred, the angel slipped in like an icy draught and smothered the firstborn of the household.

"Let my people go," said Moses. He had to raise his voice above the noise of weeping mothers, grief-stricken children.

"Go. Get out. Be gone!" said Pharaoh.

Out of Egypt streamed the Israelites, like rivulets joining into brooks, the brooks into a single river. A host of excited, happy faces hurried past the weeping Egyptian mourners, the newly dug graves. There were donkeys and carts, children and old people, women singing and men asking questions: "Where are we going? Where are you taking us, Moses?"

"To a land flowing with milk and honey," he replied, "the one God promised to Abraham." He had no more idea of the way than they had, but he had faith. Suddenly, away in the distance, a whirling spiral of darkness sprang up, like a genie, from the desert sands – a pillar of cloud. "That way," said Moses (who knew a sign when he saw one).

The pillar of cloud led the way by day, a pillar of fire after dark.

Left behind in his empty streets, Pharaoh looked out at his unfinished monuments, his empty brickfields … and seethed. "Why did I give in to that insolent Hebrew? Why did I let them go? Fetch them back," he told his army. "Fetch them *all* back!"

At the shores of the Red Sea, the war chariots caught up with the runaways. The whirling pillar of cloud placed itself between them, like a mother shielding its child, but the children of Israel had their backs to the sea and nowhere to run.

Now Moses stretched out his shepherd's staff – the one that had turned the Nile to blood – and he struck the shallow surf. Slowly, sucking and shifting the shingle, the waves writhed. Like two sleeping people rolling away from one another, the two sides of the sea rolled apart, leaving a path of glistening wet sand, rocks, starfish and weed.

The fleeing Israelites started along this corridor through the ocean glass-walled with water fifty fathoms high. They carried their children, their lambs, their bundles, held their breath between their teeth.

The watching Egyptians gaped and gasped at the sight of a sea splitting in two. Chariot horses trembled in their traces. Then the pillar of cloud vanished. *"After them, men!"* Soft sand sucked at the chariot wheels, but in the Egyptians plunged, into the heart of the hollowed sea.

"They're coming after us!" cried the Israelites, looking back over their shoulders, breaking into a run. They ran and they stumbled and they clambered out onto the sunlit stones of the far shore.

Then the walls of water crumbled, and the waves remembered to break. Like curtains being drawn closed, the two sides of the ocean rejoined. The seething foam tumbled with Egyptian wheels, helmets, reins, curses, whips, swords and prayers.

On the far side of the sea, the children of Israel lay panting on the shore. Behind them the smooth and silent sea sighed; ahead of them stretched the empty desert, humming with heat. After generations of slavery, they were finally free!

Free to do what? To go thirsty? To starve? After the happiness, panic quickly set in. The flat, hard bread they had hurriedly baked for the journey was gone now. How far must they travel to reach the land of milk and honey? "Trust God," Moses had said, but for how long?

Next morning they woke, and the ground was caked with cobwebs – or was it thistledown, or moss? Hungry little ones plucked at it and put it to their mouths. Mothers snatched it from them, sniffed the strange stuff, touched it to their tongues.

It was food.

"Eat," said Moses. "This is 'manna'. God has sent it. He has spread the desert like a table for you."

The manna would not keep. It was no good stuffing it in saddlebags or baskets, to eat the next day. By noon it had withered and shrivelled away. But each morning there was more. And so the children of Israel gradually learned to trust God's promise, day by day, to feed them, to guide them and to take care of them. ❧

"I've found a sandwich!" exclaimed the boy, looking over into the pew behind him. "Someone's left half a sandwich!" and he reached over for it.

"You can't eat that!"

"Why? Oh, is it yours? Sorry."

"No! It's not mine. But you don't know who left it there or how old it is!" He watched with disgust as the boy bit into the sandwich, but he felt compelled to ask, "What is it?"

The boy shrugged and chewed. "Manna sandwich, maybe."

THE FOREIGNER

The next morning, the boy did not come. Food poisoning, thought the old man. That sandwich. And he was angry, because he could not concentrate on the sheaf of corn he was carving. Fool boy. Even when he was not there, he could manage to make a nuisance of himself.

Then after lunch he came, his hair wet from swimming. "Didn't Jesus have any girl ancestors?" he asked, not wasting time on "Hello".

"Well, of course he did!"

"But they aren't allowed to climb in the Jesse tree, right?"

"Of course they are... in fact this sheaf of corn I'm carving right now..." The old man broke off as soon as he realized his mistake, but it was too late. He was obliged to tell the story of Ruth. ❧

Ruth was a Moabite, born in Moab, brought up with a Moabite religion. But when she married a foreigner – an Israelite living in her country – she found that she liked the thoughts in his head, the beliefs in his heart. She began to say her prayers to the God of the Israelites. Even when her husband died, Ruth did not fall back into her Moabite ways. Her greatest friend in the world was now her mother-in-law, Naomi.

Naturally, Naomi was heartbroken: her son was dead and she was marooned, penniless, in a foreign land. "I must go back home to my own people," she told Ruth. "I can't stay here with nothing to live on."

"I'll come with you," said Ruth.

"But you were born here in Moab! Your people will look after you! You don't want to be burdened with me!"

Gently Ruth took hold of the old woman's hand and laid it against her own cheek. "Wherever you go, I shall go. Your people will be my people and your God my God."

So Ruth and Naomi made the long journey to Bethlehem – two women without a man to keep them fed, sheltered, safe. They had no land to farm, no flocks to tend. In those days, life for a widow was harder than hard, and Ruth had two mouths to feed, not just one.

It was harvest time in the fields. Ruth went with the other women to glean – to pick up the ears of barley left behind by the reapers as they hacked down the crop. The spiky stubble pricked her ankles and hands; her back ached. The other women shunned her, this foreign woman, this Moabite beauty. For every grain of corn she picked up, Ruth let a tear fall.

That was when Boaz saw her; the owner of the field. He was a good, kind man. He asked about the foreign beauty weeping amid his corn – and he liked what he heard. A remarkable girl, indeed, to leave home for the sake of her mother-in-law. Boaz called her over. "When you rest," he said, "feel free to sit down with my

reapers." And he made sure that the reapers were not unkind to her and that they let plenty of grain fall as they hacked their way through the corn. Ruth told Naomi all about it when she got home that evening. And Naomi began to think what could be done.

Naomi may have had no money to share with her daughter-in-law, but she did have the wisdom of age. "I am distantly related to Boaz; he's a good man… Ruth, I want you to do exactly as I tell you…" And of course Ruth did, though the advice was astounding… and more than a little frightening.

Later, Boaz went to work on the threshing floor, pounding the ears of corn with a leather flail until they jumped like crickets. The air around him was soon smoky with dust. Threshing is exhausting work, and no sooner had Boaz eaten his supper than he curled up alongside the threshing floor and rested his head on a bale of straw. His greying hair was greyer still with corn dust, his mind busy with business and prayers. He dozed.

When he stirred, the midnight threshing floor was pitch black but for the merest moonlight. To his dismay, Boaz felt a warm weight resting across his ankles – "Who's there?" – and sat bolt upright, only to find the Moabite girl lying across his feet. Boaz blushed, and so did Ruth, though the dark hid their blushes. Her breath shook with fear, but she spoke the words Naomi had told her.

"I am Ruth, your handmaid. You are a kinsman of mine. Let me creep under your cloak and be safe."

Boaz did better. He married Ruth, and gave her and her mother-in-law a comfortable home and a place where they belonged. There were whispers among the gossips, of course. Boaz betrothed? Boaz married? And to a foreigner? But God himself had whispered in Boaz's ear. God, who had once made Eve as a helpmate for Adam, had brought to Bethlehem a wife of such courage and devotion, of such beauty and selflessness, that she would make his town immeasurably richer. The gossips were soon won round. On the day Ruth gave birth to Boaz's son, they brought flowers and little presents and broad sunny smiles. ❧

"What was the baby called?"

The carpenter pinched the bridge of his nose with finger and thumb. "You make me weary with your everlasting questions. Let me see now. Obed. The child's name was Obed."

"And what are you going to carve for him?"

The carpenter waved his chisel irritably. "Obed's not important. He just grew up to be the father of Jesse and the grandfather of –"

"At last! Jesse!" exclaimed the boy loudly, and set the church ringing. "Jesse of the Jesse tree!" The boy padded away down the church aisle. His hair was dry now. At the door he turned and called, "Obed was important, I bet! To Ruth and Boaz, I bet!"

"I didn't mean –" said the old man, but the church door banged, and he was alone. He went back to his work, but found himself saying (as if the boy were still there), "I didn't mean he *wasn't important*. I only meant that Obed doesn't have a story – written down – in the Bible. That's all I meant." And he carved a little O above the sheaf of corn – O for Obed. It was only as big as a grain of corn or a teardrop. No one would know it was there, except him. But it made him feel better, knowing he had not left out Obed altogether.

"Speak, Lord, for Your Servant is Listening"

"Be careful where you step! I put down my spectacles somewhere and now I can't find them." The carpenter was in a towering rage. His woodworking tools lay scattered at the foot of the Jesse tree: without his glasses he could not see to work. Without his glasses he could not see to find his glasses.

The boy bounded about the church, searching the side chapels and looking under the pews. "You should have a spare pair."

"Do you think I'm made of money?"

"A spare pair of eyes, I meant. What's this you're carving? It looks like Aladdin's lamp." He returned to the Jesse tree and stood rubbing it with a cuff of his sweatshirt.

"It's a cruse of oil," growled the carpenter. "In the old days, a man became king only when the high priest anointed his head with holy oil."

"So is this a story about a king or a priest?"

"What story? Was I telling a story?"

"You may as well," said the boy, making himself comfortable. "Until your glasses turn up." ❧

There was once a woman who so longed for a child that she made a deal with God. "Grant me a son, Lord," she prayed, "and I'll give him back to you!" True to her word, when Samuel was born, his mother loved him, nursed him, enjoyed and taught him… then gave him up to be a servant in the temple at Shiloh.

Eli, the high priest, was a very old man – older than I am – and blind, pretty near blind. He had sons who would take over from him when he died. But, in the meantime, he had Samuel to be his hands and eyes. Priest and boy lived out their days and nights in the temple, sleeping on the floor, in the big darkness. During the day, there was always noise – singing, chanting, the murmur of doves, the twitter of

sparrows. At night, the silence was solid black. But it held no terror for either of them. Eli's whole world was dark, and for Samuel there was the glimmer of the sacred lamp burning like a single, watchful eye.

"Samuel! Samuel!"

The boy raised himself up on one elbow. The words had awoken him. The old priest plainly needed him; perhaps he was ill. Jumping up, Samuel ran to Eli's side. "Yes, master? Here I am."

"What's the matter, child?" said Eli, bleary with sleep.

"You called, so I came."

"I did not call. Go back to sleep, child."

Samuel went and lay down again.

"Samuel! Samuel!" It was a gentle voice and very familiar. Samuel jumped up at once and hurried to Eli's side. "Here I am, master."

"I did not call," said the old priest, opening his blind eyes. "You are dreaming a lot tonight."

So Samuel went back to bed. But again the voice called to him, "Samuel! Samuel!"

Samuel felt his way through the darkness to Eli's side. "You did call, master. You did!"

Then Eli understood. "Go back to bed, child, and if the voice calls again say, 'Speak, Lord, for your servant is listening.'"

All his short life, Samuel had been trained to obey without question or quibble. He went back and laid his head down, though his eyes strained open in the darkness and his heart was jumping.

"Samuel! Samuel!" called the voice, patiently awaiting an answer.

Samuel knelt up on his bedroll. "Speak, Lord, for your servant is listening!"

And God spoke to him: out of the gentle dark, out of the glow of the sacred lamp, or out of the most distant galaxy. "I have news for Eli – bad news – and you must be the one to break it. His sons are not fit to do the work their father has done. They will not live to take his place. You are my choice, Samuel. You are the one I need."

When the voice fell silent, Samuel did not want to tell the good old man such crushing news. But the next morning, Eli was anxious to know: "What did God say to you, boy? What secrets did he entrust to you?"

Samuel was afraid that his words would kill the old man then and there, but he spoke them faithfully, and Eli nodded, fixing his shineless eyes on the shineless future. Then he patted the air with a trembling hand. "God is good," he said. "Let it come." ❧

The Jesse tree stood incomplete. Its lower branches were crowded with leaves and symbols, but the upper branches were still trapped inside the slab of oak, like something ancient and only part-unearthed.

"I see them!" cried the boy, his sharp eyes catching the glint of glass on a stone window ledge. He ran and fetched the spectacles, and the carpenter, after dabbing his eyes, crammed the glasses back onto his face.

"Shoo now!" he growled. "I've wasted enough time today. I have to get on."

"I thought it would be Jesse today," called the boy from the porch. "After the O you carved for Obed."

"O? What O? Oh, that O," said the carpenter gruffly. "Today Samuel, tomorrow Jesse." Then he wondered why he had said it. The boy would come back now for sure, expecting another story.

THE SHEPHERD KING

It was not the grief of his sons' deaths that killed Eli. In the temple at Shiloh was kept Israel's most precious treasure: the ark of the covenant. One day... ❧

"What, Noah's ark, you mean?" the boy interrupted.

"Ignorant child! This happened hundreds, maybe thousands of years after the flood." ❧

No, the ark of the covenant was a wooden box with carved angels decorating it. (What a piece of work it must have been!) It was used to hold the Ten Commandments, God's holy laws, and it was the holiest thing in all Israel. The mere sight of it made the Israelites feel invincible! Well, the hostile Philistines knew this, and when the ark was taken into battle, they attacked and captured it, knowing the loss would rip the very heart out of Israel. When Eli heard the news, he died of grief.

Samuel became priest instead of Eli's sons. As he grew older, God would often stoop down to whisper in his ear – news, commands, encouragement. It was time for Israel to have a king, said God, and Samuel was the one to anoint that king.

The man Samuel anointed first was Saul: a great man, a great soldier. Saul was like a pillar of fire leading the Israelites through every hardship, keeping them safe from their enemies.

But power does strange things to people. Saul began to forget that his crown had been given to him by God. He took no notice of Samuel's advice. Things started to go wrong. Seeing their chance, Israel's enemies closed in, like prowling wolves when a campfire goes out.

Samuel was a prophet. Not only could he hear God's voice, but he could see forward through time, as through a dazzle of light. Soon he could foresee a time when Saul would not be king. God even told him where to look for Saul's replacement: among the sons of Jesse. But which of Jesse's many sons should he choose? That was the question.

They were all fine, strong boys, tall and muscular.
They might all make good warriors in the king's
army. As Samuel met first one, then another,
then a third, no lamp flickered in his soul;
no voice spoke to him out of the farthest
galaxies, saying, "This is the one." "Are these
all the sons you have?" he asked Jesse.

"All but for David, my youngest. He's out
with the sheep," said Jesse.

David was sent for, and Samuel studied
him, like a shepherd examining a newborn
lamb… Yes. There it was. The face he had
been waiting to see. He anointed David
with holy oil – just as he might a king. "Say
nothing," he told father and son. "Not now.
Not yet."

Times were bad: the Philistines were winning
the war. David's older brothers went to fight in the
king's army, but David was too young. He was trusted
with no more than fetching and carrying. "Take your brothers these rations, David,"
said Jesse. "And come straight back."

Long before David reached the camp of King Saul, he could hear the Philistine
army jeering. Even as he handed his brothers the cheese and bread and raisins, he
could hear the sneering jibes coming from across the valley: the laughter and the
catcalls. "What's going on?" he asked.

"The Philistines have issued a challenge – their champion against ours – and
there's no one to answer it."

"Why? Is he so terrifying?" asked David.

"Have you seen him?" groaned a nearby soldier. "Tall as a horse!"

"Broad as a bull!" said another.

"Twice the size of a normal man! We don't stand a chance…"

Inside his tent, King Saul fumed with helpless rage. "Does no one dare fight this
man-mountain? Is Israel full of cowards?"

But it was not a matter of cowardice. If one brave soul was to fight Goliath and lose, then all Israel would be lost. And no one wanted to be responsible for that.

"There's a boy here, who says he will fight," said the guard at the tent doorway. It was David.

At first, Saul laughed and turned his back. But David ducked inside the tent. "Out in the fields, guarding my father's sheep, I've fought off a lion before now – wolves and bears… God helped me then. How much worse can this big bully be?"

There must have been something in the boy's face – the same thing Samuel had seen. King Saul believed him. In fact, he began to take off his armour and hang it on David's small frame: leather tunic, chain mail, a big brass helmet. David sagged under the weight, like a tree under snow. His legs bowed. "I can't wear this!" he protested. And he went, as he was, to fight the giant called Goliath.

"WHAT HAVE YOU SENT ME? A STICK TO PICK MY TEETH WITH?" roared Goliath. He cast a shadow as big as a building.

David bent down as he crossed the stream, chose a handful of round pebbles and put them into his shepherd's bag.

"DO THE ISRAELITES THINK I WILL *LAUGH* MYSELF TO DEATH?" snorted Goliath. The noise of his armour was like a cart rattling over bumpy ground. David fitted a stone into the pouch of his sling.

"COME CLOSER, BOY, AND I'LL PULL YOU LIKE A WISHBONE!" boomed Goliath. His massive feet raised clouds of dust, as if he were ablaze.

But David did not need to go any closer. He whirled his sling – it made a high, eerie whooping – then let the pebble fly.

"WELL? ARE YOU GOING TO FIGHT ME OR JUST ST–" The giant broke off, his mouth a black circle of surprise. He reeled, he staggered. His hand went up to his forehead. Then he fell. The ground shuddered.

With a single gasp, the Philistines began to run. They had lost their champion; they had lost their advantage. The Israelites went after them like cats after mice.

King Saul gazed at the shepherd boy David with admiration and joy. "From today I shall keep you by me all the time!" he declared, and hugged the boy close. Sweat from his throat trickled down onto David's hair, just like the oil used to anoint a king.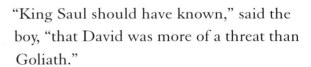

"King Saul should have known," said the boy, "that David was more of a threat than Goliath."

The carpenter looked at him sharply. "Saul was his own worst enemy. He had a dirty temper and fits of black misery. David could play the harp; sometimes that soothed Saul's dark moods. But sometimes Saul would still throw things and rant and curse like a madman."

The boy gave a lopsided sort of smile and looked firmly at the floor. "Some people are like that," he said. "They can't help it."

DANCING

A car had parked outside the church and its radio was playing very loudly – a thump-thumping rhythm which made the water in the font ripple. The boy jumped about to the music, trying to tap his bare heels together in mid-air.

"Confounded racket," complained the old man. "Stop that jigging, can't you? Remember where you are."

"Is that another rule? No dancing in church?"

The carpenter made a noise like a grumpy camel. "Humph. Do you want me to go on telling you about David or not?" ❧

Luckily, David found a good friend in the king's son, Jonathan. In fact, David and Jonathan became the kind of friends who start singing in the same key, who start speaking at the same moment. They were inseparable. Together, David and Jonathan and King Saul scythed down the Philistines like a field of corn. As the conquering army trooped home, women and girls came out to dance and sing in the streets. "Saul has killed thousands! David has killed tens of thousands!"

Over and over, Saul muttered the words under his breath. They rankled. "David... tens of thousands." Jealousy chewed on him like a dog. Suddenly the mere sight of David sitting there, plucking a gentle tune on his harp, was enough to cloud Saul's vision with red smoke. Picking up a spear, he hurled it.

David ducked. The spear hit the wall and stuck there, trembling. David fled.

Jonathan went after him. "Stop! Wait! I can talk my father around! I've done it before, haven't I?" The friends clung to each other, dreading the power and spite of the king. "Hide there, behind those rocks," said Jonathan. "Tomorrow I'll come and practise archery here.

If I shoot short, it means it's safe for you to come back. If I shoot past you…"

It did not bear thinking about: for best friends to be parted.

The next day Jonathan went out with his bow. His fingers fumbled the bowstring. His arrows flew, with a noise like sucking breath, way out over the rocks, over the crouching figure of David.

David had to leave: it was no longer safe to stay. Madness, like a raven, sat on the king's shoulder, whispering terrible thoughts into his ear. Saul now looked on David as an enemy to be hunted down and killed.

David could have fought back: he was a good enough soldier. Once he even chanced on Saul in a cave and could have killed him then and there. But David settled for slicing the fringe off Saul's cloak. "If I wanted to kill you, I could have done so today," he said, half reproachful, half taunting, "but I would never lift a finger against you."

Saul's heart was no more softened than a stone in a stream. He went to war with David, body and soul.

Faced with this madness, some of Saul's troops deserted him and went over to David's side. The Philistines, meanwhile, rubbed their hands with glee and closed in for the kill. In a disastrous battle, Saul and three of his sons were killed. One of those sons was Jonathan.

"Oh, Jonathan! Jonathan!" The cry that broke from David's throat was like a bell falling from its tower to break. Thanks to the Philistines, David had become king of Israel… and he was inconsolable.

But King David believed in God and he believed in Israel. He pulled together that unhappy, divided nation, and rode out to conquer her enemies. When the fighting was over, David determined to take the ark of the covenant (abandoned by the superstitious Philistines) to God's holy city, Jerusalem!

It had been carried into battle, stored in tents and private houses, traipsed through deserts and over mountains… Now David brought it on a brand new cart, escorted by a handpicked guard of thirty thousand men. And there were cymbals clashing, tambourines rattling, pipes and lyres and bells, and he danced and he danced… ❧

What with the music pounding on the car radio outside, the boy, too, began to dance, eyes shut, both hands raised, swaying in time to the beat.

With a clatter, the church door opened and a lady with her arms full of gladioli came in. At the sight of a barefoot boy dancing up and down the aisle, her mouth and eyes narrowed to slits. "What is that child doing, Mr Butterfield?"

The carpenter's mild reply shocked her even more: "Just dancing, Mrs Grimley. Like King David did in Jerusalem. Dancing before the Lord."

THE WISDOM OF SOLOMON

Near the cruse of oil that stood for Samuel, Mr Butterfield had carved a sling and a crown to represent King David. Close by, he carved a gateway: two pillars and a portico over the top.

"Is that David's palace?" asked the boy. The carpenter had grown so used to these daily visits that he no longer jumped when a shadow fell across his work and a small finger reached out to stroke the wood.

"It is the great Temple in Jerusalem. Solomon's Temple. You must have heard of Solomon. There were fairy tales written about him, he was so famous. Flying carpets, genies in bottles, that sort of nonsense."

"Can't you do genies, then?" said the boy, as if gates were boring by comparison.

"I'm not carving fairy stories; I'm carving *Bible* stories… At least I would be if people would just let me get on. Solomon's Temple was real." And before anyone asked him to, he was telling the story of Solomon's Temple. ❧

Solomon was David's son, but whereas David could be stupid sometimes – downright wicked on occasions – Solomon was as wise and good as any hero in a fairy tale. One day, God asked him what gift he would like best. Now you or I might have said "money" or "peace and quiet" or "long life", but not Solomon. He thought to himself, I'm a king and what do I know about anything? I'm as foolish as a little child. So he asked God to grant him wisdom. God was so delighted that he gave everything else to Solomon as well: good looks, victory, love, wealth – everything.

Out of that wealth, Solomon built a temple. God designed it, and Solomon followed the plans. Together they came up with a building so immense and beautiful that in time the world came to marvel at it. And if visitors were impressed by the Temple, they were impressed still more by the king. Solomon was a poet, a statesman and a judge from the start. It seemed as if there was no problem he could not solve.

So it was to Solomon that people brought their quarrels and lawsuits, their problems and complaints. It was to Solomon that, one day, the two women had come, thrusting the bawling baby into his face, demanding a judgement.

"She is trying to steal my baby! Tell her! Tell her she can't!"

"Don't believe a word she says! He's mine! Anyone will tell you!"

Two women. One child. Someone had to be lying. Rachel said that Miriam had stolen her baby when her own died in the night. Miriam said that it was quite the other way around. The room filled up with the feeble wailing of the baby, the swearing of oaths and the vowing of vows. Solomon put his hands over his ears. "Stop! Silence! Be still!"

All but the baby fell silent. Solomon studied the red-faced creature mewling in his lap. Then he stood up and laid the baby on the floor. Perhaps he did not want his robes dirtied.

"Are there witnesses?" he asked. There were none.

"Is there any proof or evidence?" There was only the word of the women.

"Then let the prize be shared between them!" And he called for a sword. His face was a blank, his voice as sharp and cold as a blade.

The women gaped. The king sized up the sword stroke needed – the upswing, the force, the size of the target…

Then he lifted the blade to cut the baby in two.

"STOP!" Rachel dropped to her knees and leaned across the baby to shield it with her body. "Stop! Don't! She can have him! I withdraw my claim! Only don't hurt my… Don't hurt him! Let him live!" Her eyes were like two deep wounds in her face. Miriam gave a yelp of victory.

Solomon laid aside the sword. "Now I have the evidence I needed," he said, and his voice was soft as velvet, as gentle as a woman's. Tenderly lifting the baby, he laid it, not in Miriam's reaching arms, but in Rachel's. "A child's true mother would sooner break her own heart than her child's," said Solomon. "I know now that he is yours."

The court ushers grabbed roughly at Miriam – the proven liar, the wicked stealer of babies – threatening her with fines, punishment, imprisonment. But Solomon waved them away. "Last night, this woman's child died. Has she not lost enough already?"

The court session was over. The palace fell silent, but for the distant bang and clatter of building work up at the great Temple. Solomon's soul turned inward, to that quiet inner reservoir of stillness that made him so wise. This was where he talked to God, and composed poetry about love.

Strangely enough, at the heart of Solomon's Temple, there was just such a place. People called it the Holy of Holies – an inner room furnished with stillness, where holiness itself could be found. ❧

For a long time, neither of them spoke. Then the boy said, "Solomon couldn't have been all that foolish to begin with, or he would never have asked God for wisdom, would he?"

"True."

"Did he know about you and me, old Solomon?"

Mr Butterfield narrowed his eyes. "No-o-o," he admitted cautiously. "He wasn't a prophet."

"But we know about him, right?"

"Hmm," said Mr Butterfield, scenting a trick question.

"… So that makes us wiser than Solomon, doesn't it?!" And the boy ran out of the church, laughing delightedly.

Hearing the door reopen, Mr Butterfield retaliated, "You're not wise, lad! You're just too clever for your own boots!" Then he glanced up, grinning… and saw that he had insulted the vicar by mistake.

THE IDOL AND
THE STILL SMALL VOICE

"So why wasn't Jesus a king," asked the boy the next day, "if his ancestors were David and Solomon?"

The old man examined the blade of his chisel. "Solomon's kingdom didn't last. After he died, it was carved in two by rival kings. Some time later, Ahab came to power in one of these territories. King Ahab was as wicked as Solomon was good. In fact, there was only one person in the whole world more wicked than Ahab, and Ahab married her – a woman called Jezebel." ❧

When Jezebel married Ahab, she brought her religion with her. She wasn't like Ruth. She didn't learn to love the religion of the Hebrews, the Israelites. No, Queen Jezebel chose to hate it. She set out to destroy the Israelite God and replace him with her own – the false god Baal. So the first thing she did was to order the death of every Israelite prophet: no mercy. No pity. No survivors.

But Elijah escaped the terrible slaughter. With God's help, he found himself a hiding place, like a water rat, on the bank of the River Jordan.

No food. No friends. Nowhere to turn.

Elijah curled up and closed his eyes, barely wanting ever to open them again. When he looked through his lashes, he saw black birds above him. Crows circling over a carcass, he thought.

But they were not crows. They were ravens, and in their beaks they carried bread and meat. Like small jet-black angels, they waited on Elijah. For week after week, feeding him, preserving his life. The question was: for what?

The Israelites wept. The clouds above them ought to have wept, too, at the death of so many holy prophets, but they shed not one drop. In fact, they melted away like manna at noon, and left only a brass-coloured sun that baked the country dry.

No water. No crops. Famine.

"Go to the city of Zarephath," said God to Elijah, "and do as I tell you…"

At the city gates, Elijah met a woman, thin as a stalk of corn. "Give me some water and something to eat," the prophet said.

"Me, sir?" she replied. "I'm here gathering wood to cook one last mouthful of bread. Tonight all our food will be gone, and we shall sit down together and starve, my boy and I."

But Elijah simply asked again, "Give me something to eat."

Out of charity or out of despair, the widow agreed, knowing this guest of hers would empty her flour bin and her bottle of oil once and for all.

But no! After supper, she found they were both still half full! In fact, days came and days went, and still the bin and the bottle were not emptied. "You have been good to one of God's prophets," Elijah explained, smiling at the joy a simple miracle could give.

Within weeks that joy was gone. "Is this how your great God rewards me?" The widow stood in the doorway, her little boy in her arms. The child was dead.

Elijah could find nothing to say to comfort her. He spoke to God instead. "Are you really going to let this happen to a woman who befriended me?" he implored, taking the little body in his arms, stumbling up the steps of the house. Up in his room, he laid the boy down. Three times he flung himself across the little body, berating God, pleading with God.

With a noise like a fire sucking in air, the boy began to cough, his eyes to flicker, his chest to heave. Behind Elijah, the widow laughed and wept and wept and laughed, spreading her palms to the sky. "A man of God! A man of God! Now I know you are a man of God!"

When God put life back into that little boy, he put it back, too, into Elijah. Suddenly the prophet was filled with the certainty that he could do *anything*. He was simply a tool in the hand of God (and God is a craftsman, after all).

Elijah went to King Ahab. "Abandon your idol worship! Turn back to the one true God!" he demanded. "Summon the people to Mount Carmel, and I'll show you the difference between a false god and the real thing!"

Two altars stood on the mountainside, one built by the queen's prophets of Baal,

the other by Elijah. There was no difference between them, though –
stones, sticks, a sacrificial ox – and neither was lit. The pagan
prophets began to dance and to chant, to sway and jump and roll
their eyes. "Send down fire, O mighty Baal!" they wailed. "Devour
this, our sacrifice!"

"What's the matter?" asked Elijah, after this had gone on for
a while. "Maybe Baal's asleep! Call louder!"

So the queen's prophets lunged and pranced, yelped and
whooped. "SEND DOWN FIRE, O BAAAAAL!"

No spark. No flicker. No answer.

Then Elijah raised his eyes to the sky and simply asked
once for the gift of fire.

It was as if the sun had lobbed a fireball. It was as if the
stones themselves had burst into flame. With a smell of
roast meat, a welter of orange fire swallowed up Elijah's
sacrifice. The sea of faces watching from the valley
below turned orange in the glow, then disappeared
as the crowd fell flat and cried, in one voice, "The
Lord is God!"

Elijah, his face red from the heat of the fire,
looked over at King Ahab. "Go home," he said.
"The drought is over."

From the cloudless blue of the sky, this seemed
as unlikely as… as, well, fire falling from
heaven, but Ahab had learned better than
to scoff at Elijah. Sure enough, as he
drove his chariot back to his palace,
the sky filled up with billowing
rain clouds, and sharp drops of
rain began to pierce the dust.

"Where are my prophets?"
Jezebel demanded when Ahab
returned home.

"They failed," said King Ahab.

"The true God sent fire; theirs didn't. Everyone saw."

Queen Jezebel, however, did not fall on her face and worship God. " 'Where are my prophets?' I asked."

"Elijah killed them after his God sent fire."

Jezebel's face froze over like a pond. She called for a servant and sent this message to Elijah: "May I die, too, unless I kill you within the day."

Elijah's new-found bravery melted away. He fled for his life – out of the royal city of Jezreel, out of the wet, greening countryside, out into the desert.

No food. No water. No courage.

How had anything changed for him? He was back where he had started, and so tired that he almost wished the miraculous fire had swallowed him, too, off the face of the earth.

He woke to the sound of a voice in his ear, a sweet smell of baking, a hand on his sleeve. "Eat, Elijah. Drink. Then go to Mount Horeb. God is waiting." By the time he had shaken off sleep, there was no one to be seen, but a flagon of water and a slab of cake stood beside his head.

For forty days and forty nights, that jug and cake kept him going, as he trekked across the lonely desert towards the holy mountain of Horeb. Once there, Elijah stood on the mountaintop and listened for the voice of God.

Lately, he had grown better at listening.

A blustering, bullying, bellowing wind came and buffeted the mountain, uprooting bushes, wildly wailing and whipping up the dirt… But the wind was not God speaking.

An earthquake took hold of the roots of the mountain and shook it until boulders bounced by and stones skittered downhill in landslides… But the earthquake was not God speaking.

A firestorm besieged the mountain, licking up every leaf and twig, scouring Horeb bare. Elijah was wound in a shroud of black and choking smoke… But the fire was not God speaking.

Last of all, in the silence that followed the wind and the earthquake and the fire, a calm, small voice spoke to Elijah. Elijah knew that this was the voice of God.

"Find the men called Hazael and Jehu and anoint them kings over Israel. Find the young man Elisha and teach him all you know; he must take your place when you are gone."

Elijah bowed his head. He knew he would obey. He knew that God saw far into the future – farther than any prophet – beyond wise kings and evil ones, beyond good times and bad. Elijah would go where he was sent and speak the words God put into his mouth. He was a tool, after all, in the hands of a craftsman. ❧

"Was it angel cake, do you think?" said the boy abruptly.

"Was what angel cake?" asked Mr Butterfield, confused for a moment.

"The cake that the angels delivered to Elijah in the desert. I like angel cake."

"I think it's unlikely."

"I expect those ravens were making up for the time when they didn't find any dry land for Noah!"

'They would have been very *old* ravens in that case," said the carpenter, carving the delicate feathering into a raven's wing.

"Descendants, then. Ravens from the same family tree."

"Oh, certainly," said Mr Butterfield, nodding earnestly. "Have to be, wouldn't they? Anyway, where else would you find a family of ravens, if it wasn't in a family tree? Tee-hee."

It was the closest he had come to making a joke for several years. Mr Butterfield began to whistle a breathy tune.

WAR AND PEACE

"Was Elijah one of Jesus' ancestors?"

Mr Butterfield folded his bottom lip over the top one. It was far too difficult to explain.

"Well, what about Elisha, then? Was he?"

"No, no, no. He and Elijah were prophets. Can't you see? They have a separate bough to themselves. But they often appear on Jesse trees. It's traditional."

"Why? Why are they there? If they weren't ancestors of Jesus?"

The carpenter dropped the little scraping tool he was using to hollow out the raven's eye. "It's traditional, I told you. Tradition…"

"But you must *know*," insisted the boy.

"Of course I know. Of course I do!" Mr Butterfield mopped his forehead with a dirty rag. "The prophets are there because… because they *knew* Jesus was coming. Even hundreds of years before he came, they caught glimpses of him in their dreams! They pictured him in their visions. They promised God's people that he really was coming – a redeemer, a rescuer, someone who would forgive them all their mistakes. 'A descendant of Jesse will appear…' – that's what the prophet Isaiah told them. 'A shoot will spring from the stock of Jesse and from his roots a bud will blossom.' Long before the prophets, Joseph, Moses and all the people I've told you about trusted God to rescue them. But the prophets knew something Joseph and Moses didn't. God had told them he would send a saviour. The Messiah."

"Someone to fight off their worst giants!"

"Someone to guide them back to Paradise Garden."

"So where are the prophets? Show me!"

Mr Butterfield pointed out a row of symbols dangling from one bough of his oaken Jesse tree. "Here, look. Here's one of the ravens that fed Elijah in the desert. Here's Nehemiah's trowel… (He encouraged the Israelites to rebuild the walls of Jerusalem after they were destroyed.) And here's a plough for Isaiah."

"Was he a farmer, then?"

"I told you. Weren't you listening? He was a prophet."

"I thought propheting might be a part-time job. Why a plough?"

"Because he said there would come a time, one day, when there would be no more war, and people would hammer their swords into blades for their ploughs. Imagine. Peace. Blessed peace." Mr Butterfield said it wistfully, wishfully. His head was spinning. "Next, I'll carve a bear here, to represent Elisha…"

"Ooh, a bear! Why a bear? Tell about the bear!"

The questions buzzed like hornets round Mr Butterfield's head. "Because a crowd of good-for-nothing small boys waylaid him and jeered at him and called him names and chanted, 'Go on, Baldy! Go on, Baldy!' and cheeked him and pestered him until he couldn't stand any more, so he cursed them black and blue, and two she-bears came rampaging out of a wood and ate them all up! NOW WILL YOU LET ME GET ON?!"

The boy bolted.

A moment later, the carpenter started after him, swaying unsteadily from foot to foot, arms upraised and looking very like a charging bear. "Stop! Wait!"

Clang! The big metal latch of the door clacked shut.

The bear banged up against the font, making the water slop. He steadied himself, opened the latch, but the street outside was already empty. Wearily he slumped down on a big oak chest by the door.

"I'll bet Elisha regretted that temper of his," he said under his breath. "I know I do."

The bear that he carved that day was not very fierce at all. In fact it wore an anxious sort of a smile and stood on its hind legs, stretching its neck, for all the world as if watching out for a long-awaited friend.

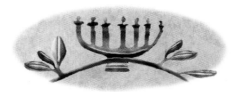

DUMBSTRUCK!

Mr Butterfield waited. He did not know what he was waiting for exactly, but he waited. Just when he finally had the chance to work undisturbed, he could not seem to get on. He had nearly reached the crown of the Jesse tree – the boughs in which he would carve the family of Jesus himself… And yet, Mr Butterfield waited, and the longer he waited, the more restless he grew. His big shoes crunched the dust up and down the aisle, and even took him up to the altar to gaze at the figures in the stained-glass windows. As the light faded behind the windows, the saints and apostles melted away. But Mr Butterfield sat down where he was, in the soft gloom, waiting.

"Are you allowed up there?" It was the boy.

"So long as I show respect," said Mr Butterfield. The bones of his knees clicked as he stood up. "Once upon a time, only the priest came past the altar rail. People aren't so strict nowadays." He waited for the boy to ask for a story. "I mean, in the Temple in Jerusalem,

only certain priests could go into the Holy of Holies, the sacred centre. It was hidden out of sight by a curtain.

"Jesus' uncle Zechariah wasn't allowed in there, even though he worked in the Temple. Zechariah loved his work, loved his wife Elizabeth, and loved living in Jerusalem. He was a man at peace – except that he had no children, and more than anything, Zechariah wanted a son." Mr Butterfield broke off.

"He was like you, you mean," said the boy. "Go on." ❧

Zechariah loved the Temple: its soft gloom, its starry candle flames, its heady scent of incense, the quiet babble of voices discussing the Scriptures. There were things in there so precious and so ancient that they crammed him topful of wonder. But when Zechariah first saw the figure standing beside the altar of incense, he was taken aback.

"Greetings, Zechariah," said the stranger with the candlelit face. "Congratulations. You are about to become a father."

Zechariah almost laughed, almost wept. All his life, he and Elizabeth had longed for a child. Now it was far too late. "Don't make fun of me. I'm old! How could…?"

But the figure cloaked in sweet-smelling smoke held up a hand. "You must call him John. He will herald the coming of the Messiah, the Saviour. He will be a voice shouting in the wilderness!"

At that, Zechariah put a hand to his throat, another to his heart, his aching, thundering heart…

The handful of people praying in the Temple looked up as Zechariah stumbled forward. His eyes were full of candlelight. His hands fluttered like doves. His mouth opening as if to speak… but no words came out. Zechariah had been struck dumb.

Even when his wife, Elizabeth, half amazed, half terrified, whispered to her husband that she was expecting a child, Zechariah could only grin and nod and scratch his joy on a wax tablet using a stylus. His writing looked like angels flying across the white wax. ❧

"So who was the stranger?" asked the boy.

"Well, bless me, an angel of course! The Angel Gabriel, at a guess. God's postman: that's how I like to think of Gabriel. I picture him, breaking the news to Zechariah, then strolling down the road to Nazareth – taking weeks about it, but whistling all the way – to speak to Mary!"

"So why didn't the angel just tell *everyone*? He could have saved himself lots of tramping about. Why didn't Angel Gabriel just roll back the sky and shout, 'HE'S COMING! THE RESCUER! YOUR SUPERHERO!' "

Mr Butterfield scratched his chin with his chisel thoughtfully. "Maybe it's not everyone who can see angels. Maybe it's only certain people."

"You could be right," said the boy with an odd smile, which he seemed to brush off with one hand and slip into his shirt pocket along with the sawdust.

MARY

"I can see it all in my head," said Mr Butterfield suddenly. "I have to work while I can picture it." As he worked, Mr Butterfield went on with the story, even though no one had asked him to. ❧

Mary was a good girl. Everyone said so. In fact, people probably never spoke about her at all, because gossips are only interested in people's faults and mistakes, and Mary did nothing wrong. She was promised in marriage to the local carpenter, Joseph. The idea pleased her, because it pleased everyone else, and happiness made Mary happy.

It was a warm day, a low sun. The olive trees wore capes of light. The herbs between her fingers gave off a dizzying fragrance. The figure in white, striding along the roadway, reflected the sun so brightly as to dazzle Mary.

"Greetings, Mary," he said. "Don't be afraid. God holds you in his mind and in his heart. I have news for you."

Mary did not jump up or run into the house. She simply greeted the stranger.

"The Lord God has chosen you, Mary, to give birth to a son. You must call him Jesus."

Mary did not faint or laugh, though her face grew paler. "How can that be? I'm not even married!"

"Mary, you're the most blessed woman alive. God's Spirit will overshadow you. He will entrust you with his own Son," said the angel. "If you are willing."

Mary did not protest or cry. She did not speak of the shame her family would feel, the things Joseph would say. She simply lowered her head. "Let it be as God wishes," was all she said.

Then the angel was gone, and so was Mary's good name. ❧

"What's wrong with the name Mary?" asked the boy. "It's a perfectly good name."

"Her reputation, I mean," said Mr Butterfield. "Mary's *reputation* was gone. After all, who's going to marry a girl who is already expecting someone else's baby? And who's going to believe a girl who says she's been talking to an angel?"

"Joseph must've," suggested the boy.

"Must he indeed? Must he?" said Mr Butterfield with an I-know-better sort of look. "If you think that, you're quite mistaken." ❧

Expecting a child?

Joseph was appalled. That spotless, devout, modest young girl everyone spoke so well of was expecting a child? The girl he was supposed to marry? Well, not any more. Joseph's chisel dug into the wood he was carving as if he were cutting Mary out of his heart. No marriage for him.

"A wife like that you can do without!" said his mother that evening, wagging her head, wagging her hands.

Then Joseph dreamed a dream. It cut into his sleep like the teeth of a saw, it was so real. It burnt through his closed eyelids and blinded him, it was so bright.

"Don't be afraid to marry Mary," said the angel in his dream. "She has done nothing wrong. The child inside her was placed there by God. He trusts her; so should you. Marry Mary."

The dream trickled out of Joseph's head like sawdust from a lathe. But the joy and the fear remained. Joseph lay on his bed staring at the ceiling. He *would* marry Mary: a woman more perfect than even he had realized. But now, of course, she would never be entirely his for, first and foremost, she and the child inside her belonged to God.

And what a responsibility! To raise and clothe and feed and educate the Son of God? A tall order for a simple village carpenter. Joseph was late opening his workshop that morning. ❧

"So he was a carpenter, just like you!" said the boy.

"Oh no, lad," said Mr Butterfield with a sad little smile. "Nothing like me. For one thing, he had a son to look after, didn't he?"

JUMPING FOR JOY

The boy pinched up some sawdust from the floor and trickled it into his shirt pocket.

"Your mother won't thank you for that when it comes to washday," said Mr Butterfield.

"She won't mind. She'll think it's sand. She says it's like the souvenir of the holiday: the sand in the suitcase… If you met an angel, Mr Butterfield, would you be happy or scared?"

"A bit of both, I suppose. A bit of each. Like Mary." And on he went with his story. ☙

Mary went to visit her cousin Elizabeth – two women, both expecting a baby, both with extraordinary stories to tell. Anyway, pregnant women always have things to talk about: names and worries, clothes and hopes, feeding and fears, sickness, birth and happiness… But even before they met – even as Elizabeth walked up the path to Mary's door – their children were already in touch.

The first Elizabeth knew of her cousin's visit was a riot of joy inside her. Her baby seemed to be leaping and kicking, like King David when he danced before the Lord! Elizabeth hurried outside into the garden, puzzled but laughing and clutching her sides. And there stood her cousin Mary, smiling.

"He knows! My baby knows! He sensed it!" Elizabeth gasped. "Mary! Mary! Blessings on you! The blessings of every mother in the world are on you now and on your unborn baby! Feel! Feel! As you came near, the baby inside me turned somersaults for pure joy!"

Mary laid her hands on her cousin's stomach. (Her own baby's movements were still too tiny to be felt.) It was like a magnet turning towards north. It was like a weathercock turning in the wind. It was like the oceans being tugged to and fro by the moon. The child in Elizabeth's womb, sensing the closeness of Mary's baby, turned in his watery world and reached out a hand. This other child was why he would struggle into the light of day. Here was his reason to live.

"Oh, Mary!" cried Elizabeth. "My baby is jumping for joy!" ❧

"That's John," said the boy. "The baby's who's leaping for joy? That's the baby who has to be called John, right? Angel's orders."

"Angel's orders," Mr Butterfield agreed. "But nobody knows that yet. Remember: old Zechariah hasn't been able to speak a word ever since that shock in the Temple…"

"Scary," said the boy, and waited.

"People fret about you when you get older," said Mr Butterfield a few minutes later. "I dare say they fretted about Zechariah."

"Because he wouldn't speak?"

"Yes, and because he was behaving oddly, too, I suppose. I'm only guessing, mind."

"It would make you behave oddly," the boy agreed. "A thing like that." ❧

Zechariah's family fretted about him, for he was old and frail. For nine months now, he had been unable to speak. They just prayed God would spare him long enough to see his son born.

But Zechariah was not sick. He had lost the power of speech, it is true, but illness had not taken it from him. God had silenced him – but he had given him something far more wonderful in return: a son.

The time came for the child to be named. The neighbours expected him to bear his father's name, but Zechariah wrote wildly on the air.

"Look!" said the neighbours. "He wants to say something! Fetch the wax tablet and the stylus."

Then Zechariah wrote, "His name is John."

Like the Red Sea splashing back onto its dry seabed, words spilled back into

Zechariah's throat. "His name is John," he said, again and again. "His name is John. His name is John! His name is John!!" Then he ran to the window and bellowed it into the street, so that a whole flock of doves flew up from the roof opposite: "HIS NAME IS JOHN!" ❧

The church rang with noise. A starling fluttered about in the organ loft. The death-watch beetles fell silent. Mr Butterfield's chisel began to peck away at the Jesse tree like a spring woodpecker. Suddenly he could picture exactly in his mind how the bough should look…

"That's my name," said the boy. "John."

"Is that a fact?" said the old man, but he was paying such attention to his work that it was hard to say if he had heard or not. Tongues of wood curled from under the tip of his chisel, as if they were shaping themselves into words. He worked on, rounding foreheads, creasing robes into pleats and folds. He worked like a man inspired. He did not notice when the boy slipped away, seeing as he did only the grain of the wood and the wood shavings falling to the ground like the moulted feathers of angels.

THE WORST OF
ALL POSSIBLE TIMES

"Seems funny," said the boy, appearing as if from nowhere. "You doing Christmas at this time of year."

Outside the church, the sun was fiercely bright. The stained-glass windows blazed blue and red and yellow, as colourful as beach huts. Fairground music floated in at the open door. "That is the next story, isn't it? Christmas?"

"It is," said the carpenter. "Daresay you don't need me to tell you any more. Everyone knows the Christmas story."

"Tell it anyway," said John, and Mr Butterfield did not put up much of a fight. ❧

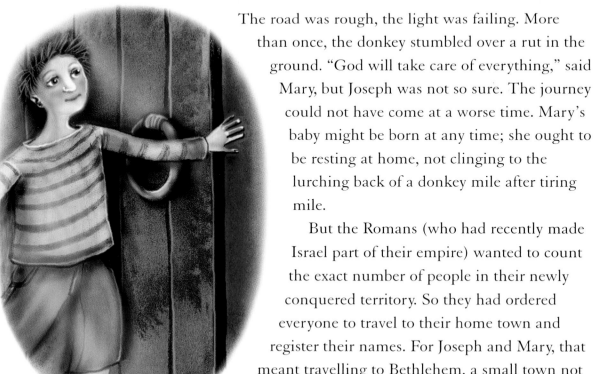

The road was rough, the light was failing. More than once, the donkey stumbled over a rut in the ground. "God will take care of everything," said Mary, but Joseph was not so sure. The journey could not have come at a worse time. Mary's baby might be born at any time; she ought to be resting at home, not clinging to the lurching back of a donkey mile after tiring mile.

But the Romans (who had recently made Israel part of their empire) wanted to count the exact number of people in their newly conquered territory. So they had ordered everyone to travel to their home town and register their names. For Joseph and Mary, that meant travelling to Bethlehem, a small town not far from Jerusalem.

The donkey pitched and rolled. As the roofs of Bethlehem came into sight, the unborn baby flexed his muscles. "It's almost time," said Mary, biting her lip.

A bed. A bed. Joseph must find somewhere for his wife to rest! But the crowds pushed past like a river breaking round an island. The town was full to bursting! Inside the clattering inn, Joseph had to shout to make himself heard. "A bed? Do you have a bed for my wife?"

"You are joking, aren't you?" said the innkeeper. "Not so much as a shelf! The whole tribe of David is in Bethlehem tonight."

Joseph's panic rose. If God really was taking care of everything, he did not seem to be making a very good job of it. "But her child! The baby! It's coming!"

The innkeeper glanced outside at the woman crouched on the ground beside her donkey. "There's always the stable, I suppose... It's not much, but it's shelter. May God be good to you both, my friend. Your baby picked a bad time to be born."

Across the yard the noise from the inn died down; its lamps went out. The only light in the stable came from a wick floating in a bowl of oil. Its flame danced in the eyes of the animals as they watched Joseph rake together a bed of straw. Their ears tilted; the flies settled on their nostrils, but they went on watching, motionless. For the woman was giving birth, and all animals understand the wonder of that. ✌

"No snow, then," said the boy. "There's always snow in the pictures."

"Probably more flies than snow in that part of the world. Flies on the cattle, flies on the donkeys, flies on the dirty straw. People mostly paint it all cosy-looking, with a row of cuddly animals. But that was the whole point, wasn't it? That the Son of God would be born in an ordinary down-to-earth place. That the Maker of the universe would squeeze himself into one, tiny, frail, ordinary, flesh-and-blood human being!

"Must've been a happy time, though. I picture the stars pulsing overhead, and the planets spinning like Catherine wheels, and the moon grinning, while the constellations did somersaults across the dark sky!"

The old man and the boy looked at one another. Both of them smiled.

"Flies have thousands of lenses in their eyes," said the boy. "They see everything thousands of times over. If there were all those flies… imagine what the flies saw, Mr Butterfield. Imagine!"

WONDERFUL NEWS

"So there was a sheep in the stable, too, was there?" said the boy. "You've carved a sheep."

Mr Butterfield held a finger against the side of his nose and winked. "Ah! You don't put sheep in a stable. This sheep was out of doors," he said.

Just up the way – outside town, beyond a fold or two of hills – some shepherds were sitting on a hillside, all huddled up in their cloaks against the midnight cold. They nodded and dozed.

Then all of a sudden, a light fell through the sky: a shooting star – that's what they thought. But the light grew bigger, formed itself into a shape, hurtled down on them, closer and closer. An eagle after the sheep! one thought, and fumbled for his slingshot.

Then the light washed over them, and the sheep glowed snowy white in the brightness, and the shepherds folded their arms over their heads and fell on their faces.

"Don't be afraid," called the figure hanging in mid-air on outstretched wings. "Wonderful news! Wonderful! The Saviour of the world is born!" The shepherds lifted first one eyelid, then two. The sheep were gazing upwards, too, yellow eyes changed to gold. "Over there! In Bethlehem! Lying in a cattle manger!" cried the angel. "Go and see for yourselves!" Within a single beat of his outspread wings, the angel was no longer alone. Others, as numberless as starlings at dusk, were there with him, hovering, silvery and singing, high over the sheepy hill: "GLORY TO GOD! PEACE TO HIS PEOPLE ON EARTH!" The singing was as loud as cheering, and there was a kind of music, too, as if someone was using the moon for a gong and was jangling all the stars.

Higher and higher the angel flock flew, shrinking to the size and brightness of fireflies. Darkness washed back again over the landscape in a flood. The sheep shuddered.

But the shepherds were already leaping and loping downhill, stumbling into rabbit holes, laughing and shouting out to one another, "Let's go and see!"

"Wait till I tell the wife!"

"Wait till I tell my children!" ❧

Mr Butterfield rested his hand on his carving of the manger. "They say the animals spoke on the night Jesus was born. But if they did, they spoke very softly: there was the baby to think of, after all…" ❧

Joseph had stuffed clean straw into the animals' feed box, and laid the newborn child in that, for a makeshift cradle. Mary was exhausted, but she didn't get much sleep that night. The baby had just been laid in the manger when the shepherds arrived. Sandals slapping in the yard, eyes still full of light, they bundled inside, noisy with excitement – then suddenly clapped their hands over their mouths, dumbstruck.

They hadn't realized it would be like this: a mucky stable, an ordinary family caught in a crisis – people just like them. The baby looked as small and as feeble as any newborn lamb. And yet for this, those angelic hosts, those creatures of light, those heavenly messengers had sung and danced across the sky, dazzling the dark!

Shyly the shepherds explained themselves, twisting their fingers into nervous knots, apologizing. Then they knelt down, before their trembling knees could give way. And their eyes and minds drank in the wonder of it – that they had been fetched by angels to see this newborn baby king. 🙠

"You tell it as if you were there," said the boy.

"While I'm carving this shepherd and his sheep, I *am* there. That's why it's such a treat and a blessing, my line of work."

"But your shepherd wasn't a relation. Jesus wasn't related to any shepherd – unless you count King David."

"Ah! but this shepherd of mine, he's not *just* the Christmas shepherd."

"He isn't?"

"No! When Jesus had grown into a man, he called himself the 'Good Shepherd'. He told a story about a shepherd with a big flock – a hundred sheep. Seems this shepherd loved his sheep so much that when just one went missing, he went out and searched and searched until he found it and brought it safe home. 'I am that good shepherd.' That's what Jesus said. He was trying to explain how he'd come to look after people – to rescue those who were lost. And whenever he explained anything, he used a story."

"So Jesus told stories, too."

Mr Butterfield was deep in thought. "Huh? Ooh, yes. He was forever telling stories! Stories about sheep, stories about parties; stories about money and friends; finding things, losing things… I suppose he grew up listening to the same stories I've been telling you, and it made a storyteller out of him. Besides… how could I leave out the shepherds? They were witnesses! They were there! They saw what happened!"

"So," said the boy. "Make me see."

THE CUNNING AND THE WISE

"Look up, then," said the carpenter, and they both bent their heads back, to examine the roof above them. High in the vaulted ceiling, the plaster was peeling and an area of black damp spread from one corner. "What's beyond the roof?"

"The sky."

"And what's beyond the sky?"

"Space. Planets. The stars."

"Exactly," breathed Mr Butterfield. "It's been the same ever since people had eyes to look. Same constellations, same galaxies. But supposing one night you looked up and saw a *new* star…"

"A supernova, you mean?"

"Or a comet, or an intergalactic meteorite skipping over the earth's atmosphere – doesn't matter which. Just suppose this brand new twinkling pinpoint of light looked you in the eye… and *winked*."

The two uncricked their necks and stared at one another. And the carpenter began a new story… ❧

Far away in the East, three astronomers uncricked their necks and stared at one another. "A new star? What does it mean?" said Caspar.

"An omen!" said Melchior, eyes full of starlight.

"Saddle the camels!" said Balthazar. "We must go and see for ourselves. Someone's been born who's going to change the history of the world!"

The three scholars took their bearings from the new star and travelled west. Their camels waded through rivers, struggled over sand dunes, spat at robbers lurking in the dark. During the day, the three sheltered from the sun and from sandstorms, biting mosquitoes, knife-edged winds. But every night they rode on, led by the star, clutching gifts for the newborn king. For surely, someone whose coming warranted

a new star in the sky must be an emperor or a king.

Riding into Jerusalem at long last, they made for the palace, of course, and explained their mission to the king who lived there. "Where is the new king whose birth we have seen written in the stars?" they asked. "We've come a long way to pay our respects to him!"

King Herod only ruled in Israel by permission of the Romans. But he clung on grimly to his crown and his throne and his little bit of power. Now, a pang of anger went through him like an arrow; he knew of no such birth. New king? New king? he thought to himself. I am the only king of the Jews!

But to the three travellers he said, "I'm afraid I know nothing of this star-child. When you find him, please come back and tell me, so that I, too, may… pay my respects." Under the folds of his robe, his fingers toyed with a dagger in its jewelled sheath. These three scholars might be wise in the ways of the night sky, but Herod had cunning enough to snuff out that star of theirs… ❧

"You'd need very long arms to snuff out a star," said the boy.

Mr Butterfield nodded. "And Herod might have been a big, important man, but inwardly he was small-minded, and small-minded people never reach the stars." ❧

Much to the astonishment of Caspar, Melchior and Balthazar, the star finally came to rest over the small town of Bethlehem. The roads were so narrow that the camels had to move in single file. Somewhere a dog barked. The three wondered if they hadn't made some terrible mistake along the way. What an exotic sight they must have been for anyone out late that night: three men outlandishly dressed, gabbling in a foreign language and pointing at the stars. What strange noises the innkeeper and his customers must have heard as they turned over in their beds: camels groaning and belching and slumping down onto their knees.

What a strange night for Mary: three dust-stained, wealthy foreigners thrusting gifts at her and the baby. What a strange discovery for the astronomers: weary, working people, a baby in a feed box, the nervy animals stepping from hoof to hoof. And yet, for this moment, fire had kindled in the distant galaxies, and careered across the night sky to announce the birth of a king!

Mary took the presents: a bag of foreign gold, a box of frankincense. (She had smelled the scent before on the hair and clothes of Cousin Zechariah after a day spent inside God's Temple.) Lastly, the visitors presented a jar of myrrh. ❧

The chisel slipped, sinking its blade into the carpenter's left palm.

"You've hurt yourself!"

"It's nothing," said Mr Butterfield. But blood welled up in the cut and fell onto his work – onto the half-carved manger. They both watched it redden the wood.

"An odd gift for a baby – myrrh," said Mr Butterfield, licking his cut. "It's for the dead, you know. An ointment used to anoint dead people... But then that's why he came, you see? That little baby. Once he was grown up, Jesus did a lot of important things. But most important of them all was dying."

They both looked up at the stained-glass window above them: a green hill, a brown cross, a man who was Jesus, spilling his blood to wash away all the wrongs in the world.

"It's like you said once," Mr Butterfield recalled. "Jesus was like the sheep who died in place of Isaac. He was like that offering on Elijah's altar. He was God's ultimate rescue plan!"

"He was like David slaying the big bad giant!"

"He was the way back to Paradise Garden!"

"He was the ram God gave to Abraham!"

Their hands brushed as they pointed to different symbols on the Jesse tree, remembering all the stories they had shared.

"He's Once-upon-a-time and The End!" said Mr Butterfield.

They sat down breathless, their backs against the trunk of the Jesse tree.

"I'm sorry you hurt your hand."

"Don't worry about it, son. Tree's all but finished, isn't it? All but done. I'll mend, don't you fret. I'll mend. But talking of blood... I haven't finished telling you about King Herod."

ANGELS

Mr Butterfield groaned as he tried to make himself comfortable. Then he began. ✿

Herod waited and waited, digging his dagger into the arm of his throne,
ruining the gilded woodwork. Where were those three astronomers? As
soon as they returned, he would know where to find that newborn
brat. He already knew how to stop it ever stealing his crown…
Tchk, tchk went the dagger's blade into the arm of his chair…
Gathering up their memories, brushing the straw off
their robes, Caspar, Melchior and Balthazar camped
outside Bethlehem and lay gazing up at the dancing
constellations. Happy and weary, they quickly fell
asleep.
Suddenly – soft as sheep's wool, white
as sheet lightning – an angel came
swooping into their dreams. "Don't go
back to Jerusalem! Don't tell King
Herod what he wants to know!
He would kill the child, not
worship at his cradle.
Go home! Go home
another way!"

So that's what they did, urging their camels into a gallop, cutting their pack mules loose. Caspar was in such a panic to obey the angel that he never stopped to wonder how Melchior and Balthazar had come to dream the selfsame dream at the selfsame moment. They simply fled, offering up prayers for that helpless little child, to the glittering, frosty stars.

The angel meanwhile turned back, flying through the dreams of all Bethlehem that night until he reached the sleeping Joseph. He had a second message, this time for the carpenter from Nazareth: "Get up, Joseph! You are not safe. King Herod wants the child dead. Make for Egypt, and stay there until the danger is past!"

So that's what Joseph did. The sight probably didn't cause much of a stir: a little family group, with their donkey, crossing an unmarked border into the Egyptian wilderness. They glanced back from time to time for signs they were being followed, but mostly they looked ahead. Hanging from the saddle's pommel were a pot of gold, a box of incense and a jar of myrrh. Cradled in Mary's arms was the Saviour of the world.

They would get by, Joseph comforted himself. God would take care of everything… And anyway, a good carpenter can pick up work anywhere. ❧

"You must carve an angel," said the boy.

"I don't know. There'll be a star – here – right at the very top."

"Oh, but you have to put in God's postman. There, look. He'll just fit, if you carve him small."

"Very well. No one seems to know how big angels are. In fact philosophers have been arguing about it for years. Just here, do you mean? As if he's in the stable?"

"Well, of course he was. All the angels went along there after they left the shepherds. Millions of them! To take a look. Wouldn't you?"

If Mr Butterfield wondered how anyone could be so sure, he was too busy to ask – too busy planning the final feature of his crowded Jesse tree.

THE BRIGHTEST STAR

"Finished!" Mr Butterfield lifted the sandpaper from the star. "The brightest star," he said under his breath. "God's brightest star."

His job of work was finished, and it pleased him. The woodcarving flourished in the church now like a living tree, its branches crowded with animals, signs and symbols. It was almost like a Christmas tree decked with ornaments, all rising towards the Christmas star. A year-round Christmas tree. A lifelong Christmas tree, you might almost say.

He wished the boy could see it. But the boy was gone. Either his holiday had ended or he had guessed the stories were at an end. "I could always have told him the *other* stories," said Mr Butterfield sadly to himself. "There are so many…" But there would be no more wet dogs, no more little brothers, no more ice creams or awkward questions, no more demands to "Tell me!"

Mr Butterfield had never thought he could miss anything so much.

There again, lots of visitors came to the church, especially in the summer: plenty of trippers, dozens of children… The thought lifted his flagging spirits.

Tipping linseed oil into a rag, he began to polish: the sitting camel, Jacob's ladder, Joseph's sandals… It was only when he came to the angel – only as he oiled the outstretched arm, the little open hand, the cheeky smile – that he saw it. It gave his heart the oddest jolt.

For there was the boy's face! Without realizing it, he must have shaped the brow, the jaw, the lips and created a perfect likeness.

Tell me, the mouth seemed to say. *Make me see!*

Mr Butterfield sat down at the foot of his Jesse tree. "Well, blow me down!" he whispered up at the glossy angel. "Who would've thought it?"

No, now he looked at it, the mouth was not *asking* for a story at all, but telling one. "Once upon a time…" To everyone who came now and stood looking with idle curiosity at the Jesse tree, wondering what stories hung ripening among its branches, this little face would speak.

If only they had the ears to listen.

"Go ahead, lad. It's your turn. Tell me. Make me see," said Mr Butterfield to the angel. "I'm listening now."

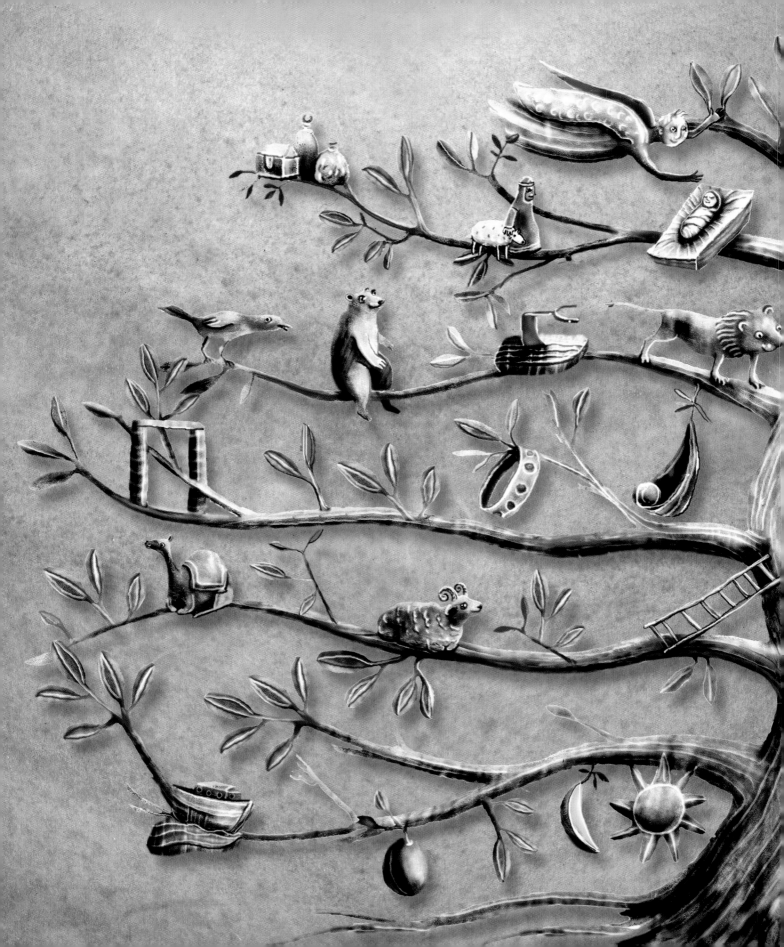

Quilt Visions 2010
NO BOUNDARIES

An Exhibition of
Thirty-nine Art Quilts

Edited by Valerie P. Stiles

Judith Content

ACKNOWLEDGEMENTS

This year, 2010, marks the celebration of Quilt Visions' 25th anniversary and the production of its 11th biennial juried international exhibition. This exhibition is possible with the hard work and valuable contributions from a large group of talented and energetic individuals. Special thanks and appreciation go to the Quilt Visions board of directors: Charlotte Bird, president; Andrea Bacal, Margrette Carr, Barbara Groner, Kristine Herman, Ann Olsen, Sheila Rideout, Sue Robertson, Valerie Stiles and Ingrid Stuiver; Phyllis Newton and Patti Sevier, past presidents; and Beth Smith, executive director.

We are grateful to jurors Jason Busch, Linda Colsh and Penny McMorris, whose dedication to the process made this exhibition possible.

We extend special recognition to quilt photographer Eric Nancarrow for his attention to detail and professional knowledge.

We are grateful to our partner, the Oceanside Museum of Art, for producing a beautiful exhibition. The staff at OMA has provided invaluable assistance throughout the exhibit process: particularly Executive Director Ed Fosmire; Director of Exhibitions and Collections Teri Sowell; Libby Tallman and Erika Koga. We also acknowledge retired Executive Director James Pahl for his many years of partnership.

Thanks to copy editors Valerie Stiles, Charlotte Bird, Jill Le Croissette, Tina Rathbone, Patti Sevier, Beth Smith and Tom Anglim.

Additional photo credits: pages 4, 6, 16–Valerie Stiles; page 9–Lisa Yoder

Graphic design: Valerie Stiles

Cover Art–*Before Sunset*, by Nelda Warkentin

Copyright 2010 by Quilt Visions

Library of Congress Control Number: 2010906748
ISBN–0972466444
Printed in China through Global Interprint

A Quilt Visions Publication
2825 Dewey Road, Suite 100
San Diego, California 92106
www.quiltvisions.org

SPONSORS

The fiber artist of today owes much to the many generous individuals and businesses that provide the tools and materials used in the works of art presented in this exhibit. The contributions of fabric manufacturers, quilt shops, guilds, artists, galleries and collectors are essential components of fiber art. Quilt Visions expresses its sincere gratitude to its valued sponsors for their generous contributions to the arts in general and to this exhibition in particular.

County of San Diego

eQuilter.com

Margrette Carr

Jill Le Croissette

Rosie's Calico Cupboard

The Warm Company

Canyon Quilters of San Diego

Friends of Fiber Art International

SEW Hut

Starseed Foundation

Julia Zgliniec, quilt appraiser

QUILT VISIONS HISTORY

This year, 2010, we are delighted to be celebrating the silver anniversary of Quilt Visions. A brief summary of the past 25 years illustrates the history and development of Quilt Visions and how it has become the organization it is today.

In the mid 1980s, the world of contemporary quiltmaking emerged in San Diego. Several active quiltmakers concluded that quilts should be recognized as art, and be displayed in museums and gallery settings. Representatives from numerous guilds met in 1985 to form Quilt San Diego. The goals of this organization included biennial exhibitions to showcase quilts, public education, and promotion of quilting as an art form.

The next few years brought non-profit status; the formation of a formal exhibition, *Visions;* and our first major fundraiser at the Lyceum Theater. The opening of the play *The Quilters* in 1989 provided important public exposure and space in the theater lobby to hang 35 contemporary and traditional quilts. The first *Visions* exhibition in 1987 was a four-day, juried show in Fallbrook, California, featuring 82 pieces. The second, in 1990, was held at the Museum of San Diego History in Balboa Park, lasting two months and representing six countries. This marked the first year Quilt Visions published a full-color catalog featuring all the quilts represented in the exhibition, and it has subsequently printed catalogs for each biennial exhibition. The exhibition moved to the Oceanside Museum of Art in 2002.

Quilt Visions has become a leader in the contemporary quilt world, attracting the best artists from all over the world. Over the years, Quilt Visions has also sponsored lectures, demonstrations, community quilts, workshops, children's programs, artist critique forums and fiber art classes.

In 2007, after 20 years of dreams, goals, planning and hard work, Visions Art Quilt Gallery opened to the public. The gallery presents approximately five new exhibits each year. In addition to this space, Quilt Visions will continue to hold its biennial exhibitions at the Oceanside Museum of Art.

Ann Olsen
Quilt Visions Past President

DIRECTOR'S STATEMENT

Oceanside Museum of Art (OMA) is thrilled to present its fifth exhibition in conjunction with Quilt Visions. The theme for 2010 is "No Boundaries" and the stunning works of art in this biennial truly explode one's notion of what a quilt can be. The variety of material, techniques and formats is magnificent. The quilts display a lively sense of freedom from convention and commonality and are so diverse in their expression that they aptly embody the theme.

The daunting task of arriving at the works of art chosen for this presentation was undertaken by a distinguished panel of jurors who reviewed 601 entries submitted by 270 artists from around the world. Winnowing the entries down to just 39 selections was a significant challenge. Of the artists represented in *Quilt Visions 2010: No Boundaries*, almost half are exhibiting with Quilt Visions for the first time.

I would like to extend special gratitude to the staff and board of OMA, including Exhibition Designer Elizabeth Tallman, Facilities Manager Erika Koga, Director of Exhibitions and Collections Teri Sowell, Assistant Director Danielle Susalla, Director of Development Natasha Bonilla-Martinez, Membership Manager Teri Ellis, Board President Beate Rüsse and Vice President Carolyn Mickelson.

The partnership that has developed between OMA and Quilt Visions over the past eight years is a collaboration of the highest order with each organization providing the appropriate expertise and resources. For that I would like to thank the staff and board of Quilt Visions, especially Executive Director Beth Smith and President Charlotte Bird. OMA is fortunate to have this superb relationship with Quilt Visions and we look forward to many more years presenting the finest in contemporary quilt making.

Ed Fosmire
Executive Director
Oceanside Museum of Art

Dinah Sargeant

SELECTION CRITERIA

The vision of *Quilt Visions 2010: No Boundaries* is that art quilting is and should be treated as a fine art, like painting and sculpture.

Artistic expression is universal, and the criteria for judging it should vary only as techniques of execution and inherent aesthetics of media necessarily vary with the materials of the artwork.

Specific goals for our jurors, as scholarly art critics, were to select work for this exhibition that reflects the universality of artistic expression and to report in their comments how this show displays art quilts in the broader contemporary art context.

Quilt Visions 2010: No Boundaries jurors:
Linda Colsh, Penny McMorris and Jason T. Busch

JASON T. BUSCH

In reflecting upon the content of *Quilt Visions 2010*, I can attest to the fact that the exhibition lives up to its moniker "No Boundaries." Indeed there are no boundaries when one considers the rich quality of work submitted of various form, scale, material, and technique. For the amateur quilter to the accomplished quilt artist, the casual culture seeker to the studied museum visitor, the work in *Quilt Visions 2010: No Boundaries* presents an international snapshot of the diverse and inspiring field of quilting. These engaging quilts stand in the face of the historic, revered form of textile that has traditionally held two primary functions, one for basic warmth and the other for conveying meaning or story behind a carefully stitched pattern. *Quilt Visions 2010: No Boundaries* makes clear for the novice (like me) as well as the informed (like my fellow jurors) that a quilt can be a powerful artistic expression for an artist, and worthy of the same level of respect and display as the other contemporary arts, whether painting, sculpture, glass, ceramic or wood. The physical composition of a quilt, which can be considered both two- and three-dimensional, uniquely positions it within the arts and with an equally compelling message or concept to those explored in other fine and decorative arts in museums today.

As a curator of historic, modern, and contemporary decorative arts, I have long admired the sense of design and technical prowess that is pro forma in creating a successful quilt. While I have never before studied contemporary quilts to the degree I did as juror for *Quilt Visions 2010: No Boundaries*, my exposure—if not immersion—to the subject during three days in Oceanside, California has instilled in me an abiding interest that will no doubt influence my work professionally. Throughout my journey, I was deeply impressed by the knowledge, experience, and critical thought process of my fellow jurors Penny McMorris and Linda Colsh, and I learned much from them. I complement Beth Smith, Charlotte Bird, and the other members of the *Quilt Visions 2010: No Boundaries* team for identifying three individuals, each of whom evaluated the works from a different perspective: accomplished quilt artist, respected quilt scholar, and art museum curator. I felt like a pupil in a quilt workshop, exposed to a vast array of complex stitching and often innovative processes that the uninitiated could take for granted (such as rusting, digital photography, and screen printing). This education crystalized for me the important master-student relationships that have undoubtedly influenced so many of the artists in *Quilt Visions 2010: No Boundaries*.

Through the provocative conversations with my fellow jurors and Quilt Visions volunteers— nearly all of whom are seasoned quilt artists and advocates in their own right—I realized we all share the same criteria that I hold standard in evaluating handmade objects: truth to materials, technique, and ornamentation; originality of design and execution; and clear and compelling meaning. These ideas consistently proved important in our selection for *Quilt Visions 2010: No Boundaries*.

JUROR

I was impressed with the overall quality of the submissions, and particularly those artists who used the physical dimensions of the quilt as their canvas—almost a foil—for a freedom of expression that was not contained by a rigid geometry. Many of the quilts exhibit the time-honored power of narration, sometimes presented in layers where the viewer is challenged to discover the message through seemingly disparate patterns, colors, and applications. One can see artists working through a series and experimenting with processes, some embracing and others completely rejecting the accepted, centuries-old ideas about quilts. I consistently found myself in admiration of quilters who are equally engaging as textile technicians and contemporary artists. And while so much of what I saw appeared to be moving in new directions for quilt art, I realized that regardless of originality or derivation, the work was moving me as an art museum curator beyond any pre-conceived notions of quilts. The artists who participated in *Quilt Visions 2010: No Boundaries* inspired me, as I consistently thought of the endless possibilities for work in the future.

I look forward to seeing the exhibition, which has a life on the walls at the Oceanside Museum of Art and a legacy in this publication. My hope, as I can imagine it is for my fellow jurors and Quilt Visions volunteers, is that the work selected here will inspire the next generation of artists to use the unparalleled form of the quilt as a vehicle for artistic expression.

Jason T. Busch is curatorial chair for collections and The Alan G. and Jane A. Lehman curator of decorative arts at Carnegie Museum of Art in Pittsburgh. Mr. Busch was formerly associate curator of architecture, design, decorative arts, craft and sculpture, and curator of the Grand Salon from the Hôtel Gaillard de La Bouëxière (Paris, c. 1735), at the Minneapolis Institute of Arts, and assistant curator of American Decorative Arts at the Wadsworth Atheneum Museum of Art in Hartford, Connecticut. He received his master's degree in Early American Culture from the Winterthur Program at the University of Delaware.

A frequent contributor of articles on museum collections and exhibitions in *The Magazine Antiques* and *Antiques and Fine Art*, Mr. Busch also has actively contributed to scholarship on decorative arts and design, culminating in several exhibitions and publications, including *Decorative Arts and Design Collections Highlights* (Carnegie Museum of Art, 2009); *Rococo: The Continuing Curve 1730–2008* (Cooper Hewitt Museum, 2008); *Currents of Change: Art and Life Along the Mississippi River, 1850–1861* (Minneapolis Institute of Arts, 2004); and *George Washington: In Profile* (Wadsworth Atheneum Museum of Art, 1999). He is presently organizing the 2012 exhibition *Inventing the Modern World: Decorative Arts at World's Fairs 1851–1939*, a collaborative project between Carnegie Museum of Art and the Nelson-Atkins Museum of Art in Kansas City, Missouri.

LINDA COLSH

Applause, applause... Congratulations to the 39 artists whose skill, mastery of the medium, and success in making compelling art rose to the top of more than 600 works entered. From the overwhelmingly strong field, we could have chosen several complete exhibitions.

The 2010 exhibition is a powerful visual statement of stitched and layered art presented in the renowned Oceanside Museum of Art. *Quilt Visions: No Boundaries* came together over three days of viewing, debating, and choosing from the many fine entries. The challenge to select a superb exhibition was serious and satisfying, involving at times some difficult choices. Whether a first time entrant or an artist with a distinguished reputation and excellent body of work, thank you all for submitting your work so that we could find the best combination of the highest caliber.

Our approach in the jury room was to look for work that was mature, fresh, evocative, moving and that worked exceptionally well as art. We gravitated to pieces by artists with something to communicate, artists who articulated an original idea with exemplary design. We looked for mastery of concept as well as mastery of craft.

We didn't ask for artist statements and were read titles only in the later rounds. Only in a few cases did we ask for a reading of the submitted list of materials and techniques. We were interested in finding the artworks with clarity of intent, where process and materials contribute without overpowering aesthetics and content. Each piece stood on its own and was evaluated for visual impact, expression of concept and worthiness as a work of art. While the three of us came to Oceanside with different art backgrounds and ideas of "what is [good] art," our approaches to determining which works to include were similar.

What I looked for was art that pulled me in initially, spoke to me, and then held my interest. I was drawn to work that resonated. I wanted to see more in the piece over subsequent viewings and went back to work that I found myself thinking about outside of the jury room. I looked for well-designed work that sparked my sense of wonder about the ideas presented, and especially art that transcended the medium.

We were keenly aware of the excellent venue where the art we selected would be presented. We repeatedly took time to visit the gallery to see the exhibition space: the lighting, walls, overall size and presentation details. We queried the installation curators about how the walls would be positioned, how viewer traffic and artwork would flow, and if there would be adequate space to view each piece up close and from a distance. We preferred work that, when displayed in this outstanding facility, would impress and give the audience pause. Interestingly, the very final choices we had to make were pressed

JUROR

by the ultimate demands of the available presentation space and optimum gallery design to do best by and for the art.

On a personal note: I thank my collaborators, Penny and Jason, for sharing your insight, knowledge and approach. To the Quilt Visions members and OMA staff, thank you all for the honor of working with and for you. In return, we give to all who visit a beautiful, stimulating, inspirational, quality *Quilt Visions: No Boundaries*.

Before the viewing, deliberations, and selections begin, each biennial Visions jury is given a charge that details the criteria for selection. In addition to asking us to treat the works as fine art, our charge concludes with the request that we report on "how this show displays art quilts in the broader contemporary art context."

As viewers experience *Quilt Visions: No Boundaries*, the assembled collection will express the exemplary state of the art quilt, and moreover, will shine the lens of the viewing public on these 39 works by artists who think beyond art quilt and focus on art. While the art quilt medium was a qualification for entry, this collection is by artists of exceptional expression and imagination who succeed in making work that exists in both worlds.

An American residing since 1990 in Everberg, Belgium, Linda Colsh has lived in America, Asia and Europe. A lifelong artist with two degrees in Art History from the University of Maryland, she exhibits in the United States and internationally and has had solo and/or two-person shows in Hungary, France, and Korea. Her award-winning art is published in numerous works including *Masters: Art Quilts*, from Lark Books, and can be found in collections worldwide. Ms. Colsh has had work in several Quilt Visions exhibitions. After having been the first European representative, she currently serves on the board of directors of Studio Art Quilt Associates.

PENNY MCMORRIS

I had the great pleasure of first jurying the fifth Visions show in 1996. So it was a distinct honor and serious responsibility to be invited back to help select quilts for *Quilt Visions 2010: No Boundaries*. (As an aside I'll mention that my fellow juror, Linda Colsh, was one of the wonderful artists exhibiting in the 1996 show.)

Now, 15 years down the road from 1996, I still find it difficult to articulate my sensations about art into words. Put another way, jurying, and writing about it, are like two different coats. I'm comfortable in one, but find the other a poor fit. And I'm always mindful of the rejected artists. Often, the line between acceptance and rejection is as thin as a thread. So here I'll focus on the selection process that led us to the quilts you'll see in the pages ahead, and admit to my biases.

Jurying took place at the Oceanside Museum of Art, during three days spent looking at slides projected on two screens (for overall view and detail) placed side by side. Each piece had a number—no artist's name. We could question the size, or ask about materials. If we felt we recognized an artist's style, we could ask if the work was by that artist.

Day one began with a silent round of slides, displaying the entire field of entries. During round two we could comment and reject work, and I felt immediately comfortable with Jason's and Linda's judgments even when we did not agree. It took three "no" votes to drop a work. With each successive slide round fewer pieces were left to reconsider, and we gained a greater familiarity with these pieces so we could judge whether we liked them more or less with each viewing.

Day two focused on winnowing the remaining group close to the magic number the show allowed. Now, to retain a work required a "yes" by all three jurors. We went through many, many rounds. On day three we made final selections, decided on prizewinners, and enjoyed one final slide go-through.

What were we all looking for during these days? Speaking only for myself, I don't strive to create a balanced show, I want only to choose the best pieces. All jurors have biases. I'll confess mine:

- Size does matter. I think the medium of layered fabric and stitching usually works best on a large scale. It is not a delicate medium, so I find it hard for small quilts to really have any impact. I'm always yearning for more.

- "If it walks like a duck and quacks like a duck but is not a duck." If your work reminds me of Nancy Crow, but you're not Nancy Crow, I can't help but be influenced

JUROR

negatively. I want your style to come from you and your life. So if your work reminds me too strongly of another artist it's next to impossible to view it as a fresh new idea.

- I need to see good photos. Bad photos indicate a lack of professionalism.

- Details matter—I want to focus in on the main event in your piece.

- If you submit more than one piece, but each looks like the work of a different artist, I sense you've not yet developed a cohesive style.

- I'm often wanting less, not more. In a field where so many works are brightly colored, with busy abstract compositions layering mixtures of stitching and varied materials, I'm often looking for a quieter voice, someone working more minimally: reducing, not adding.

- I don't care what the subject matter is—it's how you deal with it.

This show exhibits the work of some current masters alongside up-and-comers who appear to have a long career before them. It was a pleasure and honor to be involved with it, working with Linda and Jason, and the efficient and personable Quilt Visions team, led by Charlotte Bird. Congratulations to all of the artists, not only those accepted, but all who entered. Would that you all could understand how much we enjoyed your work even though we did not have space to include it.

Penny McMorris was the corporate art curator at Owens Corning Corporation for 20 years. She curated one of the first contemporary quilt shows in the country in 1976. In 1986 she co-authored *The Art Quilt*, the first book focusing on quilt design development. She was the American consultant for the British Craft Council's "Contemporary American Quilts" exhibition in London in 1993, and was guest curator for the 1988 "Homage to the Quilt" exhibition, and the 1992 "Nancy Crow: Works in Transition," both at what was then The American Craft Museum in NYC. She helped form the contemporary quilt collections of Ardis and Robert James, now part of the International Quilt Study Center Collection, and that of John Walsh III. She produced and hosted three PBS television series on quiltmaking and is currently vice-president of The Electric Quilt Company, makers of software for quilters.

QUILT VISIONS MISSION

Quilt Visions is a not-for-profit international arts organization dedicated to the promotion and appreciation of the quilt as art. Two major activities achieve this mission:

- The biennial international juried exhibition, *Quilt Visions 2010: No Boundaries*, presented at the Oceanside Museum of Art, Oceanside, California. This is the 11th Quilt Visions exhibition.

- The Visions Art Quilt Gallery presents exhibitions and education programs, showcasing the finest in contemporary art quilts and fiber art.

Judith Larzelere

AWARDS

The **Quilts Japan Award** rewards the artist whose work will encourage and inspire quilt artists internationally. It is awarded by Japan Handi Crafts Instructors' Association and Nihon Vogue Co. Ltd. to Velda Newman for her quilt *Zinnia*.

The **CREAM Award** (Cathy Rasmussen Emerging Artist Memorial Award) is awarded by the Studio Art Quilt Associates (SAQA) to an artist with a work in a Quilt Visions exhibition for the first time. This year's award is presented to Dianne Firth for her work *Road Across the Mountains*. The CREAM Award is so named in memory of SAQA's first executive director. The 2010 award is made in memory of Eva Henneberry.

The **Friends of Fiber Art International Award** is given to Sharon Bell for *Waterfall* as the quilt which most reflects the universality of artistic expression.

The **Surface Design Association Award** is presented for work which exemplifies the Surface Design Association's mission to inspire, encourage and further the rich tradition of the textile arts through the creative exploration of coloring, patterning and structuring of fiber and fabric. It is presented to Rachel Brumer for *Small Regional Still Lives*.

The **Sponsor's Award** is given by Rosie Gonzalez to Joan Sowada for her work *Flight Zone*. The award is an acknowledgement of artistic ability and is intended to encourage artists to explore more fully the medium of the art quilt.

The **President's Choice Award** is chosen by the president of Quilt Visions. Charlotte Bird selected *River Notes* by Judith Plotner.

The **Brakensiek Caught Our Eye Award** is presented to Valya for her piece, *Cell Memory. BABA.* Nancy and Warren Brakensiek are longtime contemporary art quilt collectors living in Albuquerque, New Mexico. They believe that a collector's eye can be different from that of professional judges or experts.

Quilt Japan Award
Zinnia by Velda Newman

Brakensiek Caught Our Eye Award
Cell Memory. BABA by Valya

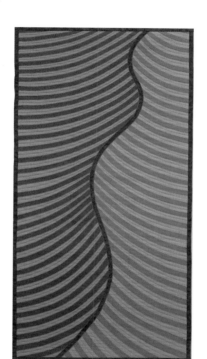

SAQA CREAM Award
Road Across the Mountains
by Dianne Firth

Sponsor's Award
Flight Zone by Joan Sowada

Friends of Fiber Art International Award
Waterfall by Sharon Bell

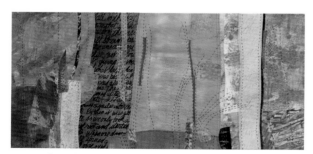

President's Choice Award
River Notes by Judith Plotner

Surface Design Association Award
Small Regional Still Lives by Rachel Brumer

Anne McKenzie Nickolson

QUILT VISIONS 2010: NO BOUNDARIES
The Quilts

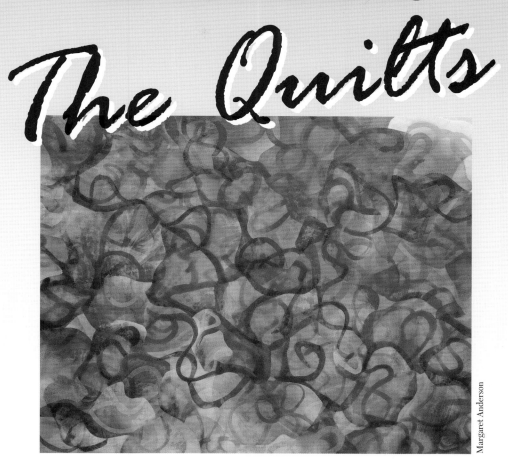

Margaret Anderson

Deborah Bein

21

Deidre Adams

Littleton, Colorado USA

My work is primarily about texture and color, using the concepts of time and external forces as a creative starting point. I use the textile medium, fabric and stitch, because it imparts a unique texture, both visual and literal to my work while imparting a physical reminder of the artist's hand. Patterning and texture from the base fabrics interact with stitched lines and my own system of painting and mark-making to create a richly layered surface. Although abstract in design, my work often includes elements evocative of structure, with vertical and horizontal divisions reminiscent of windows and doorways.

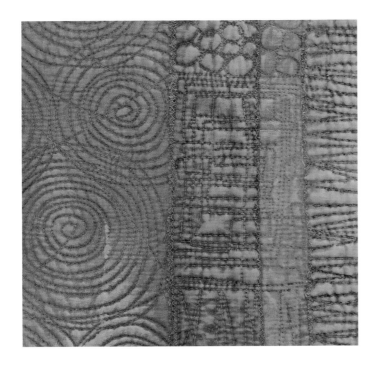

38 x 63 inches

Cotton fabrics, batting, acrylic paint

Machine stitched, hand painted

Façade VI

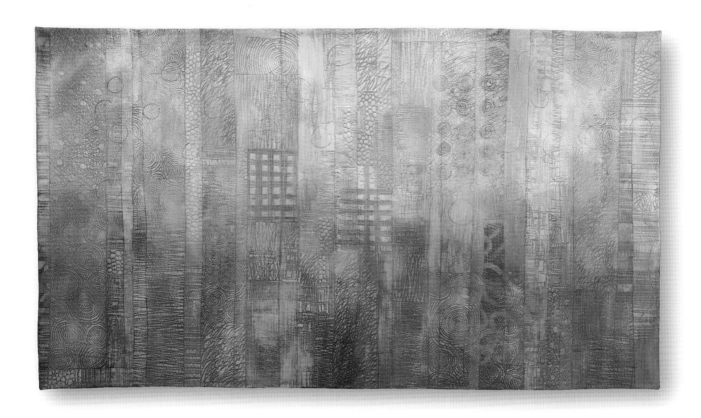

Pamela Allen

Kingston, Ontario Canada

For three millennia, Eve has been branded the original sinner for partaking of the fruit of the tree of knowledge. She has received most unfair criticism in my opinion. Eve brought knowledge and therefore understanding, compassion and empathy to our lives. No wonder she needed to share with Adam!

45 x 42 inches

Recycled and commercial fabrics, upholstery trim, Styrofoam® fruit

Big stitch, raw-edge appliquéd; machine free-motion quilted and drawn

Wanna Bite?

Margaret Anderson

Sedona, Arizona USA

I approach my abstract designs intuitively and with
a sense of adventure. As I spontaneously build layers
of collage, my ideas gradually become increasingly
defined until the final design emerges. *Curvilinear*
is an example of the visual texture and complexity I
enjoy creating in my work.

39 x 39 inches

Acrylic painted silk, polyester batting,
cotton backing

Painted on silk, collaged, hand
appliquéd, hand quilted

Brooke Atherton

Billings, Montana USA

The journey thus far. taking stock, making sense. Am I the person I meant to be?

41 x 45 inches

Found clothing (silk, synthetic); silk organza, found objects

Rusted, dyed, burned, pieced, layered, stitched by hand and machine

Barbara Barrick McKie

Lyme, Connecticut USA

One of the most beautiful birds I have seen, a Crested Barbet, visited our lunch at our camp in Botswana and inspired this quilt.

29 x 44 inches

Disperse dyed polyester printed after computer manipulation, rayon thread

Free-motion thread painted, machine appliquéd and quilted, trapunto on non-regulated sewing machine

Crested Barbet

Linda Beach

Chugiak, Alaska USA

Slow and unstoppable, a tree can thrive amidst granite boulders.

37 x 60 inches

100% cotton commercial fabrics, cotton batting, cotton and synthetic threads

Machine pieced, free-motion machine quilted

Tenacity

Polly Bech

Swarthmore, Pennsylvania USA

Cracks in the rock, a sign of things beginning to change.

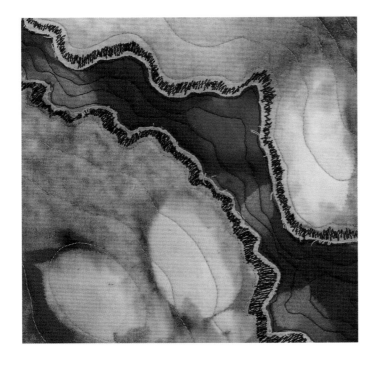

30 x 52 inches

Solar-printed cotton, printed by the artist

Machine pieced and machine quilted

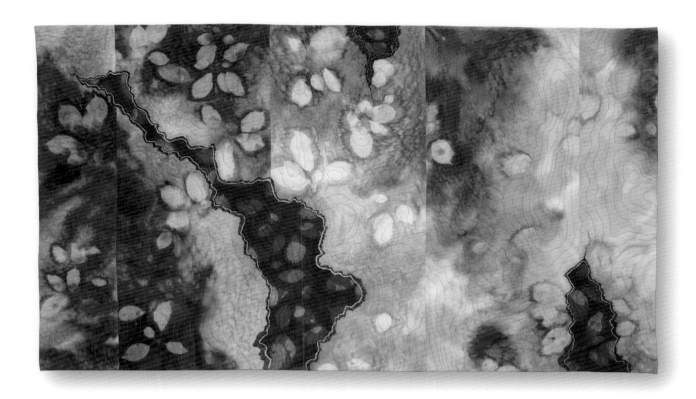

Deborah Bein
Poughkeepsie, New York USA

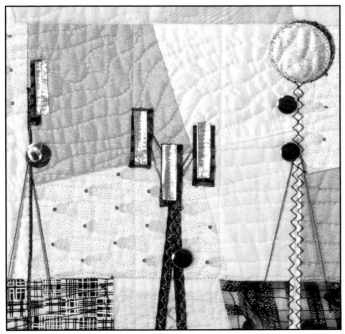

30 x 70 inches

Commercial fabrics (cotton, satin, corduroy, heat reflective/insulation fabric, metallic-laminate), thread, and embellishments (plastic jewels, duct tape, sequins, ribbon), ink

Pieced, quilted, fused, machine appliquéd, glued, inked

Oh Say Can You Cell

The trashing of the great American landscape for the sake of constant contact.

Sharon Bell

Shaker Heights, Ohio USA

Capturing the beauty, complexity, and simplicity of the basic elements continues to challenge. The elements of art are used to suggest a waterfall using repetition as cascading water.

67 x 20 inches

Archival ink, cotton face, back and batting, cotton thread

Whole cloth quilt, hand quilted and lettered by the artist

Rachel Brumer

Seattle, Washington USA

I solicited a small sample of people living in Seattle to work on this still life project with me. I asked them to collect objects that held meaning or memories. These images are parts of those still lives. The creation of this work was supported in part by the Jentel Foundation of Banner, Wyoming, and by an Artist Trust Fellowship of Seattle, Washington.

55 x 83 inches

Hand dyed cotton, cotton batting, thread, commercial cotton backing

Van Dyke printed, hand appliquéd, hand quilted

Betty Busby

Albuquerque, New Mexico USA

Push is a visual representation of my interest in molecular biology. The growth of organisms involves processes of movement, attachment and change, and I have abstracted these processes in this work.

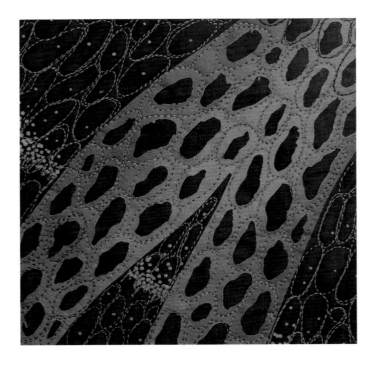

44 x 37 inches

Silk, non-wovens, paint

Hand dyed, hand painted, burned, appliquéd, thread painted

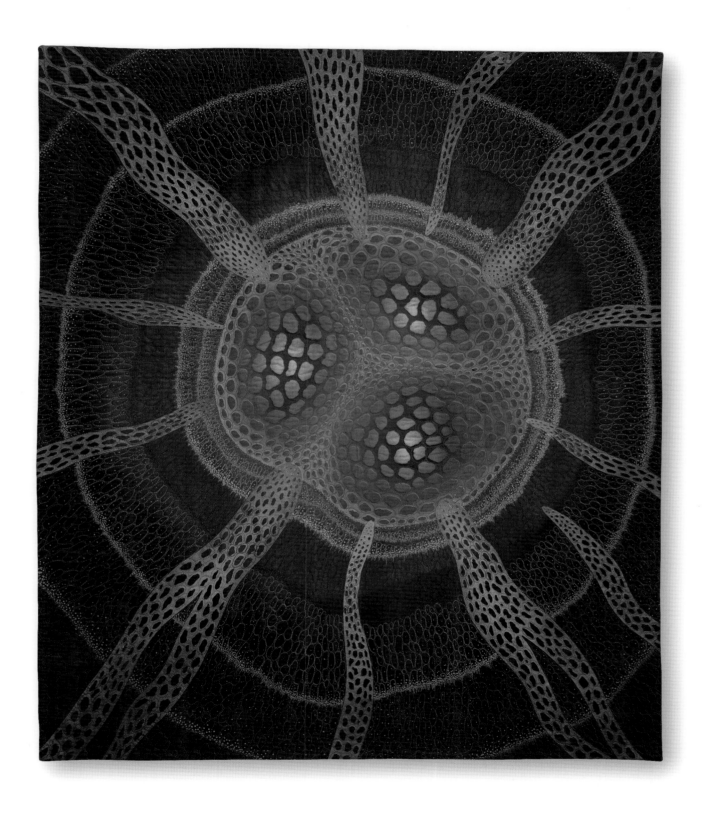

Elizabeth Busch

Glenburn, Maine USA

hot, cold
bones, flesh
in front, behind
fear, faith
chaos, calm
where to go

41 x 47 inches

Cotton canvas, textile paint,
commercial fabric, poly batting,
cotton back, embroidery thread,
Prismacolor pencil

Machine pieced, hand painted, hand
quilted by the artist

Benedicte Caneill

Larchmont, New York USA

The *Units* series explores the construction of a whole piece using elemental geometric units that, when joined create an abstract composition with lines, colors and movement. I design my own fabrics through the monoprinting process, cut those fabrics and as I reassemble them an imaginary composition emerges reflecting my vision of nature. *Units 21: Jungle Fever,* is an evocation of the jungle with the colors of birds, flowers and the sun filtering through luscious foliage.

38 x 38 inches

Cotton fabrics monoprinted by the artist, fabric paints, MX dyes, polyester batting, cotton backing, cotton and polyester threads

Monoprinted fabric using textile paints on Plexiglas® plate, hand cut, machine pieced, free-motion machine quilted, hand drawn designs

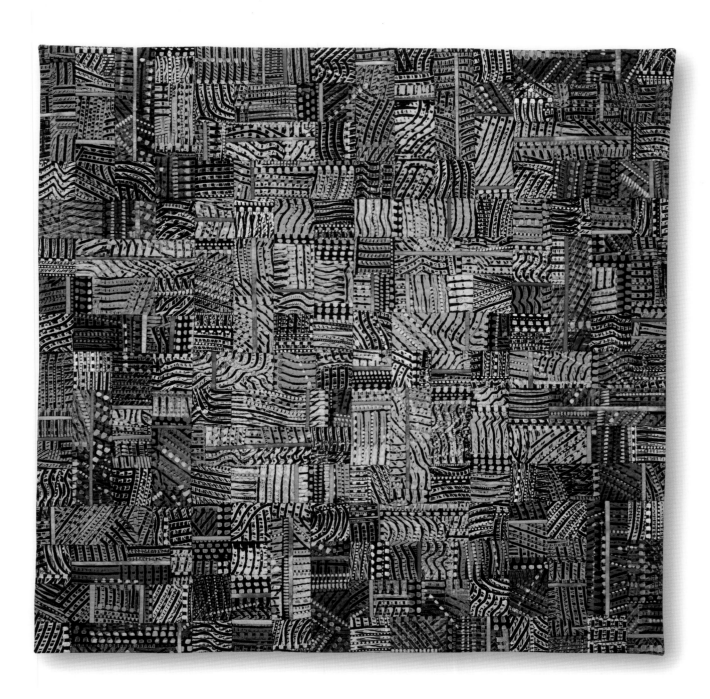

Sue Cavanaugh

Columbus, Ohio USA

Ten miles west of Taos, New Mexico, a bridge crosses 650 feet above the Rio Grande. This piece celebrates the power, majesty and wonderment of water, time and creation. What path does a human life forge on its journey? How often do we push past the imaginary banks that limit our choices?

50 x 64 inches

Cotton sateen, fiber reactive dyes, micro-cord, cotton and silk floss, thread, cotton batting, cotton backing

Whole cloth, stitch resist shibori patterned, dye painted (multiple times), hand stitched

Ori-Kume #14: Rio Grande at Taos

Jette Clover

Antwerpen, Belgium

In my current series, *White Walls,* I am moving into a quieter and more subdued space and exploring the psychological and symbolic possibilities of the non-color white and the principle of 'less is more.'

I am printing letters and text in black and then erasing it again and creating a ghost image by over-painting many times with white acrylic paint and sanding certain areas to reveal what is beneath the surface. Afterwards I will add small fragments of torn posters in red or yellow to this whitewashed wall.

53 x 56 inches

Cotton, acrylics

Painted, screen printed, collaged, hand and machine quilted

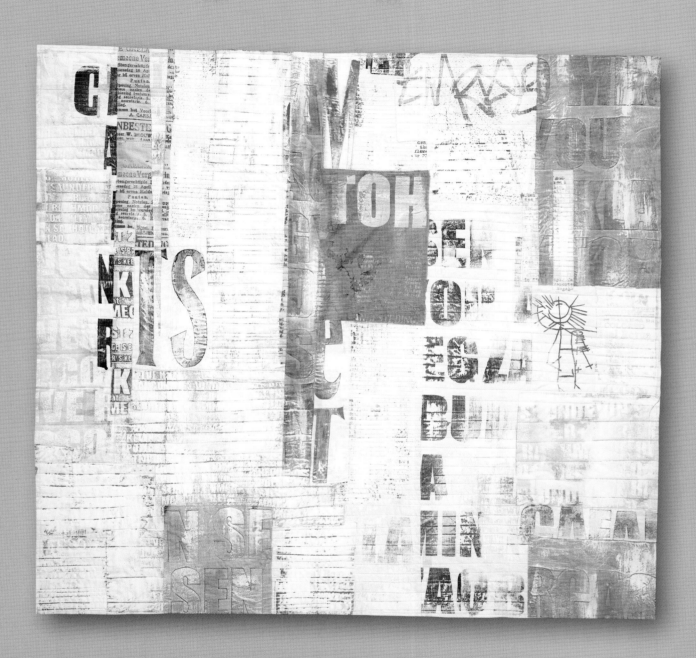

Nancy Condon

Stillwater, Minnesota USA

This piece was inspired by the many times I look in the mirror and see an old woman; sometimes my mother, my grandmother and others. The composite of overlapping photos taken over several days is an attempt to resolve those images with the self inside.

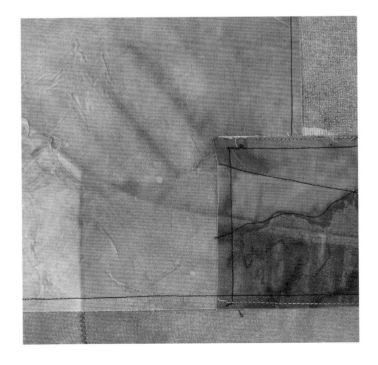

61 x 29 inches

Fused polyester organza, found clothing fabric, hand dyed cottons, silk, inkjet images printed on the fused fabrics

Photo imagery printed on fabric, multiple passes, fused layers using fusible web between layers, Photoshop® manipulation of imagery

Self Portrait After Middle Age

Judith Content

Palo Alto, California USA

This piece was inspired by the cataclysmic eruption of Krakatoa in 1883. Heard almost 2,000 miles away, the eruption caused devastating tsunamis and darkened the sun throughout the world. When the volcanic ash began to dissipate, glorious sunsets lit the evening sky.

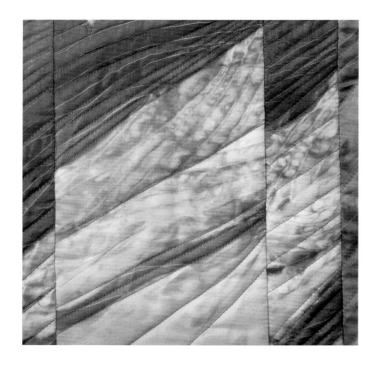

55 x 85 inches

Silk satin, thread, cotton/poly, raw silk

Shibori dyed, pieced, machine quilted

Dianne Firth

Canberra, ACT Australia

Mountains provide a physical boundary that often divides regions. Access routes, such as roads, break down this division and provide new opportunities for people and places.

74 x 29 inches

Commercial cotton, polyester batting, polyester thread

Pieced, torn-strip appliquéd, machine quilted

Road Across the Mountains
SAQA CREAM (Cathy Rasmussen Emerging Artist Memorial) Award

Britt Friedman

Oberlin, Ohio USA

This quilt is one of a series of quilts that I have made of grasses. The inspiration is the elegant, graceful forms of grasses. This piece was designed using combined and transformed elements from several of my photographs. The work requires an often lengthy process of experimentation and visual discovery, which perhaps best resembles painting or writing poetry, with elements being added, subtracted, adjusted and readjusted. I would like my subject matter to be recognizable but not literal. I want it to express my own viewpoint and experiences of nature while at the same time resonating with and providing pleasure to the viewer.

25 x 60 inches

Polyester, cotton

Artist's photographs, printed, machine quilted

Gloria Hansen

East Windsor, New Jersey USA

My work is about geometric shapes and visual ambiguities. I create it by merging digital and traditional media with textiles and quilt making. This can include using computer programs as design tools with or without my photographic imagery, printers to help create printed cloth, and various surface design tools and techniques with paints, pastels, and traditional media to further the work.

40 x 57 inches

Silk, pigment ink, colored pencils, pastels, cotton, textile paints

Digital painting and photo collage printed on silk with archival ink, colored pencil and pastel, machine stitched and quilted

It's Time

Jane LaFazio
San Diego, California USA

Eucalyptus pods and leaves fractured by cutting into bits, chunks and squares. In this case, reassembled and overlaid with circles to become nearly whole again if only in memory. A Zen meditation and tribute to the giant, regal, scented eucalyptus tree with its colors of taupe, celadon and plum.

48 x 36 inches

Hand-made felt, dyed cotton batting, paint, embroidery threads

Hand sewn, needle felted, hand dyed

Zen Eucalyptus

Judith Larzelere

Westerly, Rhode Island USA

I continue to explore strip piecing and strip quilting to develop new ideas. I have come to feel that the value of my work is visual; it does not have an explanation.

64 x 60 inches

100% cottons, front fabrics hand dyed by Heide Stoll Weber, back commercial cottons, batting polyester

Machine strip pieced, machine strip quilted

Static Interference

Anne McKenzie Nickolson

Indianapolis, Indiana USA

Much of my current body of work uses images from the world of painting that are inserted into my structured, layered textiles. Originally, the painted images were chosen because of the painters' particular attention to the painting of fabric. More recently, I choose images that persistently resonate with me. My original goal was to return the figures to the world of cloth, but more and more, I want to present emotionally powerful images to my viewers.

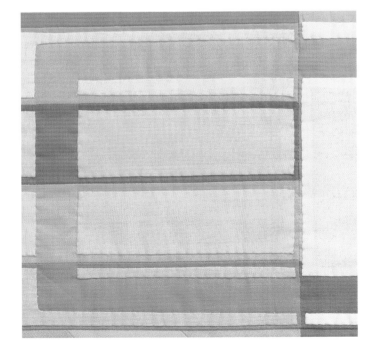

57 x 56 inches

Commercial cotton broadcloth, cotton batting

Machine pieced, hand appliquéd through all layers

Velda Newman

Nevada City, California USA

87 x 212 inches

Cotton sateen

Hand dyed cotton sateen, paint, ink

Hand appliquéd and quilted, painted, inked

Zinnia
Quilts Japan Award

I find nature to be an endless source of inspiration and my life on the shores and in the mountains of California has influenced me most. I begin conventionally by breaking down a design into its most basic elements of shape and color. However, somewhere in the process my vision skews—colors become bolder, shapes and subjects get larger. It is through this use of exaggerated colors and shapes that I hope to inspire the viewer. Color and composition are essential elements in my designs, but the greatest emotional and aesthetic impact comes from their larger-than-life scale.

Katie Pasquini Masopust

Santa Fe, New Mexico USA

I enjoy painting to music, in acrylic, onto thin weight canvas. I then cut up those canvases and reconstruct them into a pleasing pattern. This is then turned into a quilt and then the painting is stitched into the quilt.

40 x 69 inches

Cottons, blends and ultrasuede, acrylic painted canvas

Turned-edge machine appliquéd, machine quilted

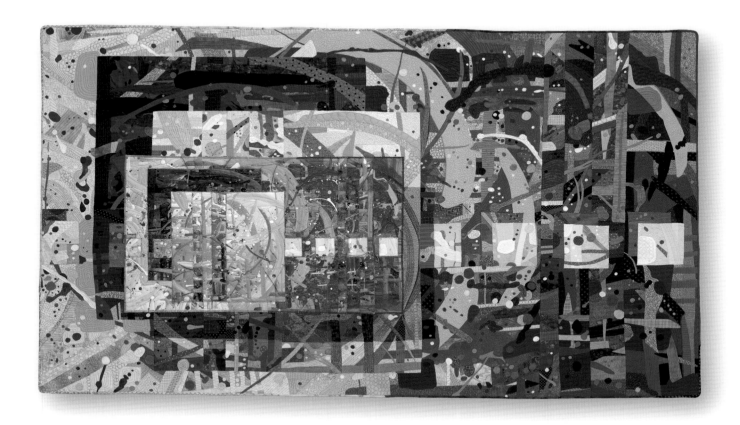

Judith Plotner

Gloversville, New York USA

River Notes was inspired by a kayak trip on Fall Stream in the Adirondacks. Integrating my training as painter and printmaker with my love of fabric and collage and using thoughts and symbols, I work using a stream of consciousness thought process. I try to portray the essence of my experience, incorporating fragments of written messages on my hand dyed and monoprinted fabric.

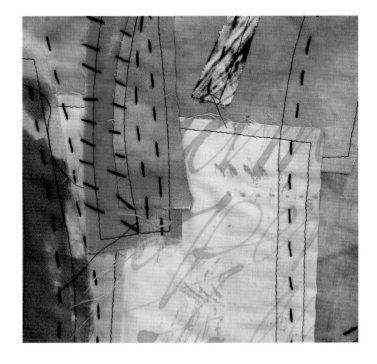

25 x 51 inches

Hand dyed cotton, cotton batting

Painted, dyed and monoprinted cotton, silkscreened, machine pieced and appliquéd, machine and hand quilted

River Notes
President's Choice Award

Sandra Poteet

Grass Valley, California USA

The inspiration for this piece was lying around as a scrap of old batting. I was looking at it and it occurred to me how such an important part of a quilt is never seen. So what if it was on the outside? Then we could see what really goes on...in the batting.

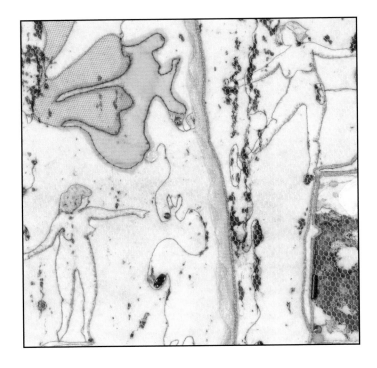

67 x 37 inches

Cotton batting, tulle, scrap cottons, synthetics, hand woven yarn, inks, beads, yarn, and wood

Machine and hand appliquéd, machine quilted, couched, hand beaded and ink stained

In the Batting

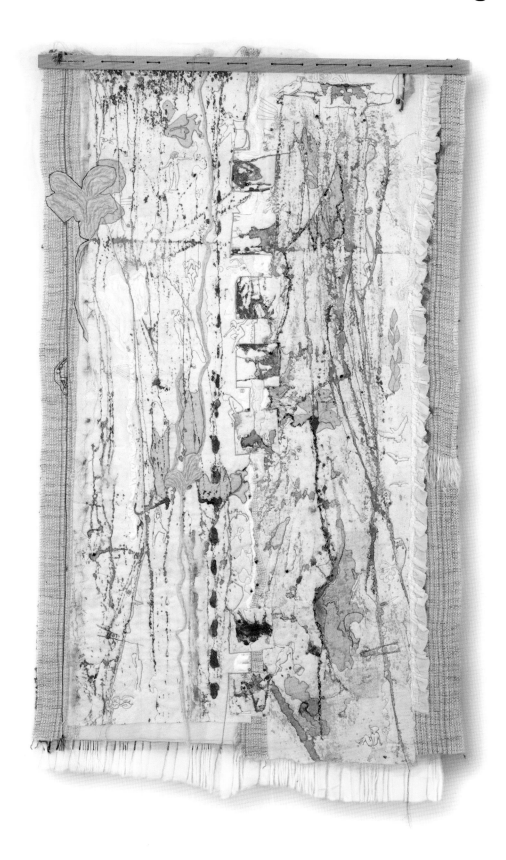

Dinah Sargeant

Newhall, California USA

The voice calls back.

An ancient song,

returns to greet me.

58 x 65 inches

Hand painted cotton, fabric paint and resist, acrylic paint, ribbon, cotton batting

Raw-edge appliquéd, turned-edge hand appliquéd, machine quilted

Echo

Joan Schulze

Sunnyvale, California USA

Contemporary life is so complicated and layered. I am trying to make sense of it in collage form.

36 x 45 inches

Silk, paper

Glue transfer processes, collaged, stitched, machine quilted

Patti Shaw

Seattle, Washington USA

I like to think there is good in all human beings so
I decided to put together a group of what I imagine
to be kindhearted people.

54 x 37 inches

Muslin, pen, paint, fusible interfacing,
thread, metal clips

41 portraits–each 4 x 6 inches
hand drawn, machine stitched

Kerby C. Smith and Lura Schwarz Smith

Coarsegold, California USA

Graffiti is a lively art form. The ebb and flow of spray paint covering a wall outside the Chris Sorensen Studio in Fresno has been the focus of Kerby's point-and-shoot camera for a couple of years. The images of paint, texture and details like nail heads have provided prints, fabrics and quilts. In this piece Kerby collaborated with Lura, producing a synergetic work in the series.

The challenge for artists who normally work independently begins with mutual respect. It allows the team freely to exchange ideas as fabric gets pushed around on the design wall. Lura suggested the cascade of orange squares down along the blue V of paint to convey the ephemeral nature of paint layering of the wall.

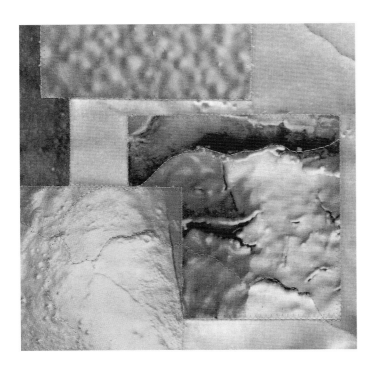

41 x 41 inches

Digitally printed cotton fabric, other cotton fabrics

Digital images printed on cotton fabric with Ultrachrome HDR inks, machine appliquéd, machine quilted

Joan Sowada

Gillette, Wyoming USA

These young men are tapped into the source. They have found a perfect harmony of movement with their skateboards and with the conditions of the day, making it look easy to those of us who are watching. For this image I have chosen fresh colors and abstract shapes for the background, hoping to convey the light air and warm sun. I took reference photos in Portland, Oregon at a skateboard competition.

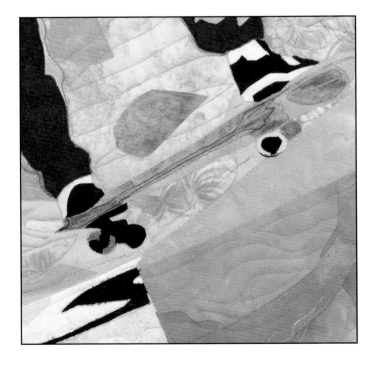

52 x 49 inches

Commercial fabrics, oil pastel sticks, markers

Fused, raw-edge machine appliquéd and machine quilted

Valya

Oceanside, California USA

This quilt is one in a series that addresses the concept of cell memory and the idea that DNA can unlock the secrets of human ancestry.

109 x 79 inches

Merino fleece, netting

Wet felted, hand quilted with a felt needle

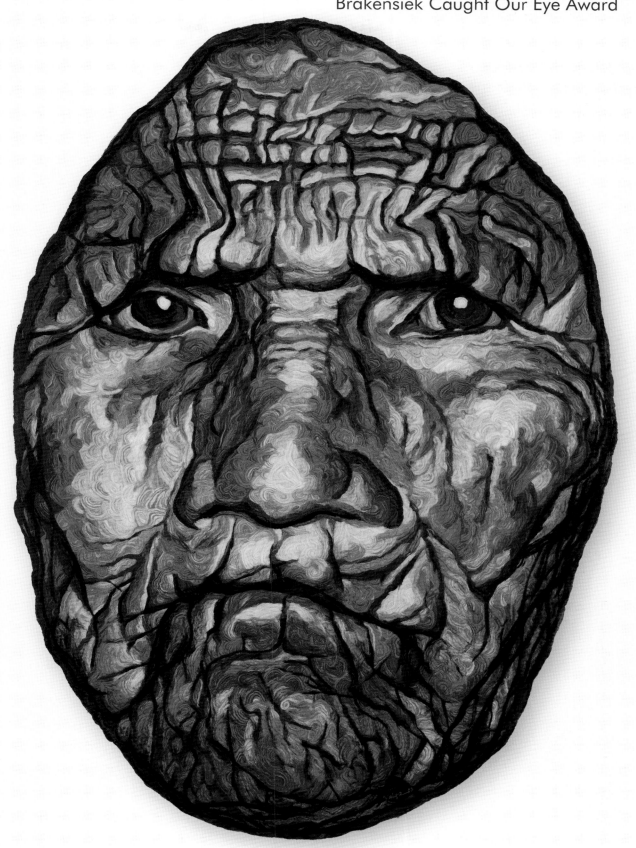

Nelda Warkentin

Anchorage, Alaska USA

The evening sunlight coming through the woods highlighted the geometrical lines.

14 x 50 inches

Multiple layers of acrylic painted silk over painted cotton and canvas

Painted, layered, machine constructed and quilted

Before Sunset

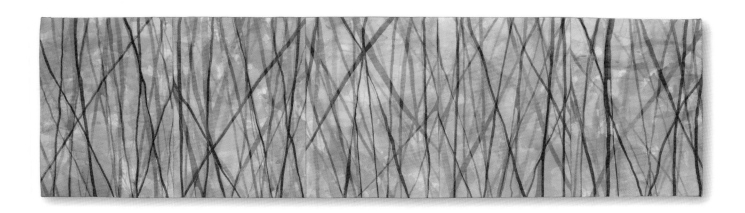

Martha Warshaw

Cincinnati, Ohio USA

This quilt is in the form of a flattened generic house (end walls, side walls, roof) whose sections are printed with patterns made using the work of an unknown quilter. It has to do, in part, with comfort, and with the way new comes from old.

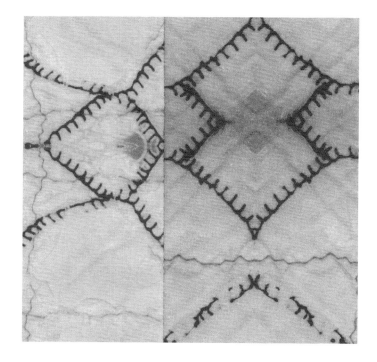

30 x 30 inches

Fabric designed (by artist) using photographs of a worn quilt (quilter unknown), printed cotton fabric

Inkjet printed, machine pieced, tied

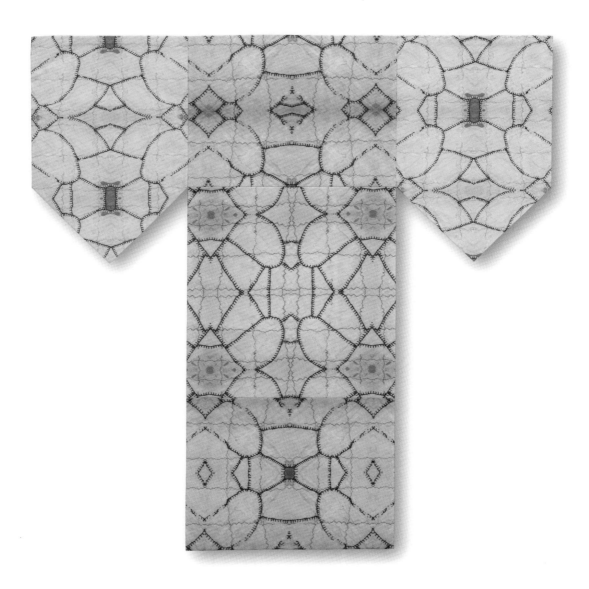

Kathy Weaver

Highland Park, Illinois USA

Several years ago I was diagnosed with a rare cellular disease. While much of my work addresses the intersection between technology and art, artificial intelligence and robotics, this life-changing event forced me to examine life at a cellular, nano-scale.

Strategic Alliance portrays an alternative world where details are shown on a macro plane. The forms have as source material artificial intelligence and draw from photographic and microscope scans of simple-celled plants and animals. I use a bird's-eye view, multiple levels and large forms to explore the environment from a nano robot's perspective. The interiors show an unearthly, intriguing and threatening world and represent the life source, the spark in the primordial soup from which we evolved. In these stitched mixed media works, the environment is devoid of overt action, yet is filled with the premonition of surprising behavior.

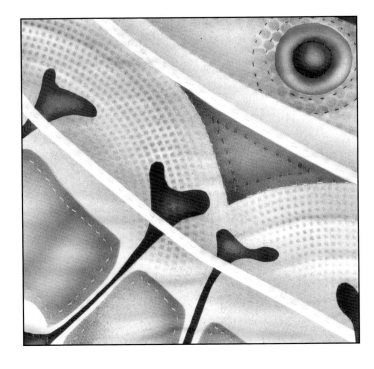

48 x 56 inches

Satin

Airbrushed, hand quilted

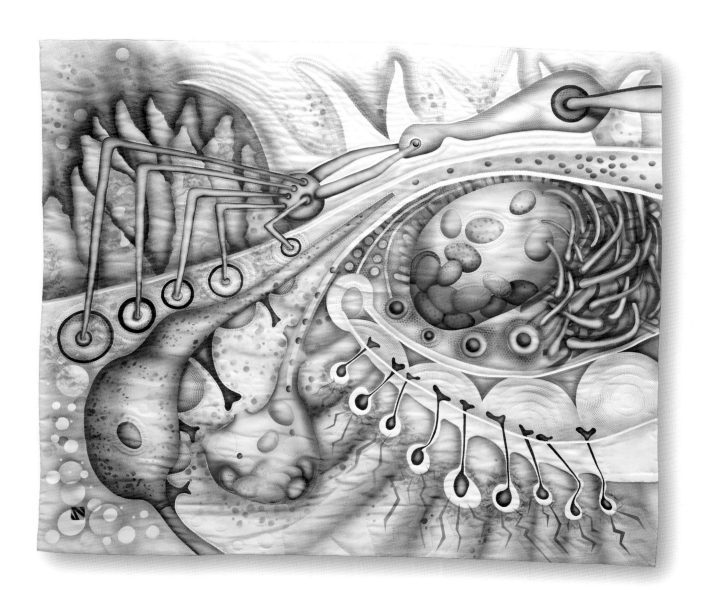

Susan Willen

Redondo Beach, California USA

We humans are set down in the midst of seemingly
unintelligible complexity—art is a way to try and
make sense of it all.

46 x 68 inches

Commercial and hand dyed cotton
fabrics, printed and discharged from
thermofax screens, rayon and cotton
thread

Pieced and machine appliquéd

Kent Williams

Madison, Wisconsin USA

I've been meaning to start a new series based on the American flag and the country for which it stands, but I keep getting distracted by line, color, shape, texture, life, liberty and the pursuit of happiness.

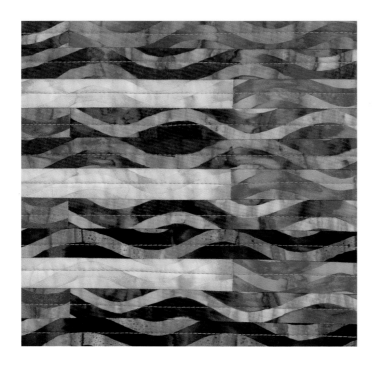

57 x 59 inches

Cotton fabric, cotton thread

Machine pieced, machine quilted

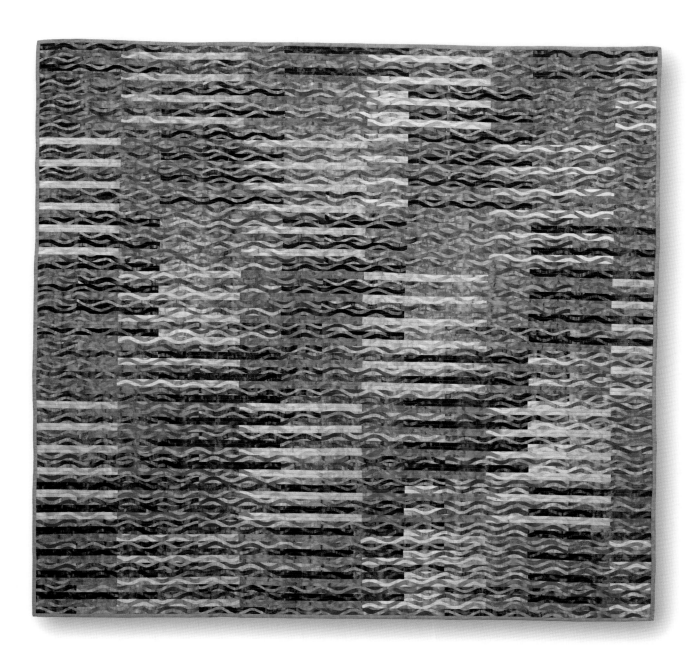

Maria Winner

Portland, Oregon USA

If you are lucky enough to have been able to float down the Colorado River through the Grand Canyon, the experience will stay with you forever. Besides all the fabulous whitewater, camping and hiking, for me it is the light. The light between the walls does incredible things.

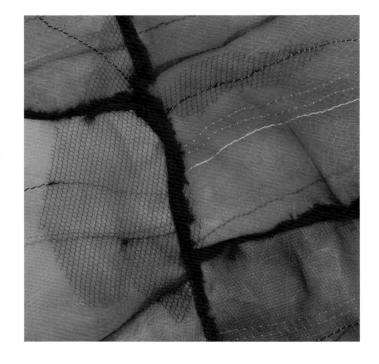

33 x 23 inches

Hand dyed Indian cotton, hand dyed silk organza, frayed rayon seam binding, hand and commercial dyed tulle, rayon machine thread

Hand dyed, layered, piece quilted, machine embroidered

INDEX